The Skylark of Space

E. E. "Doc" Smith

Illustrated by O. G. Estes Jr.

Introduction to the Bison Books
Edition by Vernor Vinge

UNIVERSITY OF NEBRASKA PRESS
LINCOLN

© 1928 by Experimenter Publishing Company
© 1946, 1947, 1950, 1958 by Edward E. Smith, Ph.D.
Introduction © 2001 by the University of Nebraska Press
All rights reserved
Manufactured in the United States of America

First Bison Books printing: 2001
Most recent printing indicated by the last digit below:
10   9   8   7   6   5   4   3   2   1

Library of Congress Cataloging-in-Publication Data
Smith, E. E. (Edward Elmer), 1890–1965.
The skylark of space / E. E. "Doc" Smith; illustrated by O. G. Estes Jr.; introduction to
the Bison Books edition by Vernor Vinge—Commemorative ed., Bison Books ed.
p.   cm.—(Bison frontiers of imagination series)
ISBN 0-8032-9286-4 (pbk.: alk. paper)
1. Space flight—Fiction.   2. Space ships—Fiction.   I. Title.   II. Bison frontiers of
imagination.
PS3537.M349S56   2001
813'.54—dc21
00-051190

This Bison Books edition follows the original in beginning chapter 1 on arabic page 5; no
material has been omitted.

VERNOR VINGE

Introduction
A New Manifest Destiny

Edward E. "Doc" Smith (1890–1965) began writing *The Skylark of Space* in 1915 and completed the novel in 1920.[1] The work first appeared in *Amazing Stories* in 1928. This Bison Books edition is a reprinting of Doc Smith's 1958 revision of the novel. *Skylark* counts as an early space adventure. To my knowledge, it is one of the very first interstellar adventures.

Skylark has appeal right from the first page, even the first paragraph. We are confronted with an experimental result that is utterly surprising and points to miracles—if only we can study it more. As with many science fiction stories, *Skylark*'s opening revolves around a miracle substance. This happens in the genre so often that there is even a generic name for it: unobtainium. But Doc Smith gives a good reason for the rarity of his X, a reason that amounts to the anthropic principle.

Throughout the book, we share with Seeton and Crane and DuQuesne a feeling of empowerment, the notion that engineering and intelligence are levers to ever greater success. As long as the reader can suspend disbelief, such a story can be a marvelously entertaining experience. It can be a difficult business kidding the reader into suspending disbelief. For myself, the gadgeteering remained entertaining right through the end of the novel. The *Skylark of Space* was followed by three sequels, *Skylark Three*, *Skylark of Valeron*, and *Skylark DuQuesne*.

The last sequel, *Skylark DuQuesne*, was probably written after 1960. I've browsed these books and found that the successive trumping of earlier technologies is less engaging than in the first of the series. Beyond a certain point, high technology becomes so successful that there must be consequences that affect the basis of the characters, ultimately the basis of human nature—and I don't see these consequences in the series. Nevertheless, Doc's *Skylark* novels touch on many ideas that are staples of science-fiction stories in 2000.

Some readers judge the quality of past science fiction by the successful predictions they find in the stories. (This normally means "successful predictions relative to the opinions in the era of the later reader.") There is another measure of quality, sometimes in conflict with successful predictions: How faithful is the story to what science was known at the time the story was written? For the most part, Doc Smith sidesteps these two measures. His story focuses on things that can't be easily extrapolated from twentieth-century technology. We do have an encounter with a dark star that behaves a lot like a black hole. But earlier, when we discover that faster-than-light travel is possible, Seeton dismisses relativity with pragmatism: "Einstein's Theory is still a theory. This . . . [faster-than-light behavior] is an observed fact." This works for me! It is when an author makes an entirely concrete statement that there can be unequivocal factual dissonance (for instance, in Doc's conflation of acceleration and velocity).

The most interesting character in *Skylark of Space* is the human villain, Marc DuQuesne. He loves science and technological progress. He would like to see civilization prosper. Thus DuQuesne has many interests and values that coincide with those of the story's "good guys," Seeton, Crane, and Vaneman. In some situations he works as their ally. At the same time, he is their frank and deadly enemy. Marc DuQuesne balances all things in relation to how they benefit him. He comes close to the nineteenth-century egoist ideal, though a true egoist might seek Seeton and Crane as long-term allies. Interestingly, DuQuesne is the title character in the last novel in the *Skylark* series.

It is a commonplace of science fiction literary criticism that each science fiction story is a mirror of the times in which it is written. Certainly a story that was truly unrelated to the mindset of the current market would be a hard sell. But each of us lives in our own context, and so the mirror can distort in marvelous ways.

If *Skylark of Space* fell into the hands of future archeologists, they might actually use it as a telescope on early twentieth-century America. Take Smith's treatment of women. Even before the rise of feminism, science fiction had a reputation for inept treatment of gender relations. Someone once said, "Science fiction in the early days wasn't sexist, it was neuter!" In fact, whatever pronouns were used, the personalities were vaguely like early adolescent males. This is not precisely the situation in *Skylark*. In fact, Doc Smith may have gotten himself into more trouble with later critics because he *did* try to incorporate something about women in his story. The original magazine edition of *Skylark* and the 1946 book edition list a co-author, Lee Hawkins Garby. According to John Clute, Mrs. Garby was enlisted by Smith to make the female character aspects of the story more realistic.[2] And yet in *Skylark* (at least the 1958 version), women are strictly separated from men in all intellectual interests and in almost all personality characteristics. Dorothy Vaneman is plucky but not grandly heroic. She is an accomplished musician but otherwise seems to be completely absorbed with home management and boyfriend/husband support. Child-raising is not an issue in *Skylark*, but a kindly interpretation of the Seeton/Vaneman relationship would be the "specialized partnership" model of marriage. Of course, this model is used by supporters of male tyranny (at least when they feel the need for intellectual justification). But in fact, this point of view is also held by many couples who do have something like an equal but specialized partnership. For the time in which *Skylark* was written, this role for women might have been mildly enlightened; it's even possible that Mrs. Garby was behind it.

It would be interesting to use such past science fiction stories to probe *our* present. Pose some questions. For instance, what is the most disturbing thing in a story? For me, the most disturbing thing in *Skylark* is the good guys' attitude toward the Kondalonian civilization of the planet Osnome. The Kondalonian policy of eugenics via execution is presented in mildly approving terms. In adventure science fiction, at least that before 1950, ideas like this were common. For example, enemy races were often so evil that they were exterminated (perhaps with the claim' that the defeated enemy would refuse to accept anything less than a fight to the death). I believe that such genocidal fantasies, paradoxically enough, sprang from innocence. Science fiction is a genre of hyperbole: the largest city, that fastest spaceship, . . . the most evil aliens. Few science fiction writers before 1945 had local examples of how closely this last trope matches the language of real, monstrous villainy. (Norman Spinrad makes a brilliant, mocking parody of this type of science fiction in his novel *The Iron Dream*, in which, in a parallel universe, a young Adolf Hitler emigrates to the United States and becomes a science fiction writer.[3]) Since World War II, of course, cautionary tales abound. But I am confident that if modern writers were brought up in the context of the first half of the twentieth century, they would have the same blind spots. This should warn us all to examine what our ideas mean when they are acted out in the real world.

There are other aspects of Doc Smith's context to consider, aspects more local and of greater creative effect. In *Skylark of Space* I see the popularity of Thomas Edison, the idea that experimentalism leads inevitably to important advances. There is the idea that mathematics and engineering can dramatically and quickly exploit the discoveries of the experimentalists. There is also the notion of manifest destiny, or at least the Yankee enthusiasm for expanding into new frontiers. At the same time, there is an awareness that the universe is a big place, so big that the theological fantasies of the past might have a reality Out There. This combination yields an exploration story with a new flavor: the "savages" of Doc's unknown worlds may be our technological and mental superiors.

Playing out manifest destiny on an interstellar stage is an interesting—some would say an impossible—exercise. And yet Doc Smith manages it. Many space adventures of the twentieth century have carried on the tradition of human manifest destiny. There are various mechanisms to achieve this incredible result. Most commonly, humankind learns that even though we aren't the smartest creatures in the universe, we are young and energetic. We are smarter than the crudely violent races, and we will learn from and displace the decadent and ineffectual elder races. Some of these mechanisms are near the surface in *Skylark* (see the encounter with the mind creature in chapter 15).

It is interesting to follow the Human Manifest Destiny trope through the twentieth century. Editors such as John W. Campbell strongly encouraged it, but the idea had a life of its own as well. Later in the century, stories such as Damon Knight's "Rule Golden"[4] and my own "Original Sin"[5] turned manifest destiny on its head. An obsessive application of "science fiction is only a mirror of the current times" might link these later stories to current events (say, the Vietnam War in the case of "Original Sin"). More likely, the contrarian stories are simply a reaction to the preponderance of the manifest destiny viewpoint. In a sense, the contrarians then are just another distortion of the mirror. (This sort of thing reflects and reflects, leading to stories such as Harry Turtledove's "The Road Not Taken."[6])

Even if one believes that Doc Smith's writing was simply a product of his cultural context, that context was something new. *The Skylark of Space* was one of the first stories in a new subgenre, and it reflected a new attitude about humankind's place in the larger universe. Being out in front is an interesting place for a writer, with its special advantages and disadvantages. Like the first persons to visit a beach strewn with diamonds, such writers need only reach out to fill their work with precious gems. Almost everything they do is original and sparkling. But a downside lurks for the writer at such a beginning—there is no body of prior art. There is no standard to compare with, and the writer is often excused from standards that apply in collateral genres. At first glance, these facts may seem to be *advantages*, giving freedom to the writer. But of course, it is often the constraints that drive art—and those constraints are much loosened at the birth of a new genre.

Looking back at these beginnings from the turn of the new century, it is very easy to be smug. We have a hundred years of intense discussion, much cross-pollination, and an enormous body of science fiction stories before us. A thousand story angles have been exploited, and the commercial competition has become steadily more intense. The art of writing about technological progress is understood at a very high level by many writers who *also* have the skills associated with the former mainstream. Nowadays we have a midden of cultural knowledge for our literature that is one hundred years deep. That is the great advantage of writing late in the life of an art form. Of course, the great disadvantage for writers at this end of the genre's life is that we have hashed and rehashed the issues, reflected and re-reflected. We are building nuances on top of nuances to the point where some of what we do is just a head game, and the refinements are in danger of becoming empty noise.[7] There is one important thing that protects the genre. Unlike many others, ours depends on external change. As long as that change continues, we may have the ability to transform ourselves. And some of the technological changes that are on the horizon are so extreme that they may transform our art and our selves into beginners once more.[8] I think Doc would be pleased by where things are going.

NOTES

1. John Clute and Peter Nicholls, eds., *The Encyclopedia of Science Fiction* (St. Martin's Press, 1993).

2. Clute, *Encyclopedia.*

3. Norman Spinrad, *The Iron Dream* (Avon Science Fiction, 1972).

4. Damon Knight, "Rule Golden," in *Three Novels.* 1954. (Doubleday and Co., 1967).

5. Vernor Vinge, "Original Sin," *Analog Science Fiction/Science Fact,* December 1972.

6. Harry Turtledove, "The Road Not Taken," *Analog Science Fiction/ Science Fact,* November 1985.

7. Gunther S. Stent, *The Coming of the Golden Age: A View of the End of Progress* (The Natural History Press, 1969).

8. Vernor Vinge, "The Coming Technological Singularity" (paper presented at the VISION-21 Symposium, sponsored by NASA Lewis Research Center and the Ohio Aerospace Institute, Cleveland OH, 30–31 March 1993). A slightly changed version appeared in the Winter 1993 issue of *Whole Earth Review.*

Foreword

To any profound thinkers in the realms of Science who may chance to read this story, greetings:

I have taken certain liberties with several more or less commonly accepted theories, but I assure you that those theories have not been violated altogether in ignorance. Some of them I myself believe sound, others I consider unsound, still others are so far out of my own line that I am not well enough informed upon their basic mathematical foundations to have come to any definite conclusion one way or the other.

Whether or not I considered any theory sound, Mrs. Garby and I did not hesitate to disregard it if its literal application would have interfered with what we considered the logical development of the story. More, we plead guilty to two extravagances each so nearly mathematically impossible that there can be set up against its occurrence a probability greater than any assignable value, however great.

I am not apologizing for these things. I am explaining them and hoping that, since you already realize how little of a fundamental nature we really *know*, you will not allow them to interfere with whatever enjoyment you may get out of the story.

Edward E. Smith, Ph.D.

THE SKYLARK OF SPACE

chapter **1**

PETRIFIED WITH ASTONISHMENT, RICHARD
Seaton stared after the copper steam-bath upon which, a
moment before, he had been electrolyzing his solution of
"X," the unknown metal. As soon as he had removed the
beaker with its precious contents the heavy bath had jumped
endwise from under his hand as though it were alive. It had
flown with terrific speed over the table, smashing a dozen
reagent-bottles on its way, and straight on out through the
open window. Hastily setting the beaker down, he seized
his binoculars and focused them upon the flying bath, which
now, to the unaided vision, was merely a speck in the distance.
Through the glass he saw that it did not fall to the ground,
but continued on in a straight line, its rapidly diminishing
size alone showing the enormous velocity at which it was
moving. It grew smaller and smaller. In a few seconds it
disappeared.

Slowly lowering the binoculars to his side, Seaton turned
like a man in a trance. He stared dazedly, first at the litter
of broken bottles covering the table, and then at the empty
space under the hood where the bath had stood for so many
years.

Aroused by the entrance of his laboratory helper, he silently
motioned him to clean up the wreckage.

"What happened, doctor?"

"Search me, Dan. . . . wish I knew, myself," Seaton replied, absently, lost in wonder at what he had just seen.

Ferdinand Scott, a chemist from an adjoining laboratory,
entered breezily.

"Hello, Dicky, thought I heard a rack—Good Lord! What
you been celebrating? Had an explosion?"

"Uh-uh." Seaton shook his head. "Something funny—
darned funny. I can tell you *what* happened, but that's all."

He did so, and while he talked he prowled about the big
room, examining minutely every instrument, dial, meter,
gauge, and indicator in the place.

Scott's face showed in turn interest, surprise, and pitying

5

alarm. "Dick, boy, I don't know why you wrecked the joint, and I don't know whether that yarn came out of a bottle or a needle, but believe me, it stinks. It's an honest-to-God, bottled-in-bond stinkeroo if I ever heard one. You'd better lay off the stuff, whatever it is.

Seeing that Seaton was paying no attention to him, Scott left the room, shaking his head.

Seaton walked slowly to his desk, picked up his blackened and battered briar pipe, and sat down. What could *possibly* have happened, to result in such shattering of all the natural laws he knew? An inert mass of metal *couldn't* fly off into space without the application of a force—in this case an enormous, a really tremendous force—a force probably of the order of magnitude of atomic energy. But it hadn't been atomic energy. That was out. Definitely. No hard radiation . . . His instruments would have indicated and recorded a hundredth of a millimicrocurie, and every one of them had sat placidly on dead-center zero through the whole show. What was that force?

And where? In the cell? The solution? The bath? Those three places were . . . all the places there were.

Concentrating all the power of his mind—deaf, dumb, and blind to every external thing—he sat motionless, with his forgotten pipe clenched between his teeth.

He sat there while most of his fellow chemists finished the day's work and went home; sat there while the room slowly darkened with the coming of night.

Finally he stood up and turned on the lights. Tapping the stem of his pipe against his palm, he spoke aloud. "Absolutely the only unusual incidents in this whole job were a slight slopping over of the solution onto the copper and the short-circuiting of the wires when I grabbed the beaker . . . wonder if it will repeat. . . ."

He took a piece of copper wire and dipped it into the solution of the mysterious metal. Upon withdrawing it he saw that the wire had changed its appearance, the X having apparently replaced a layer of the original metal. Standing well clear of the table, he touched the wire with the conductors. There was a slight spark, a snap, and it disappeared. Simultaneously there was a sharp sound, like that made by the impact of a rifle bullet, and Seaton saw with amazement a small round hole where the wire had gone completely through the heavy brick wall. There was power—and how!—but whatever it was, it was a fact. A demonstrable fact.

Suddenly he realized that he was hungry; and, glancing

at his watch, saw that it was ten o'clock. And he had had a date for dinner at seven with his fiancée at her home, their first dinner since their engagement! Cursing himself for an idiot, he hastily left the laboratory. Going down the corridor, he saw that Marc DuQuesne, a fellow research man, was also working late. He left the building, mounted his motorcycle, and was soon tearing up Connecticut Avenue toward his sweetheart's home.

On the way, an idea struck him like a blow of a fist. He forgot even his motorcycle, and only the instinct of the trained rider saved him from disaster during the next few blocks. As he drew near his destination, however, he made a determined effort to pull himself together.

"What a stunt!" he muttered ruefully to himself as he considered what he had done. "What a stupid jerk! If she doesn't give me the bum's rush for this I'll never do it again if I live to be a million years old!"

chapter **2**

AS EVENING CAME ON AND THE FIREFLIES began flashing over the grounds of her luxurious Chevy Chase home, Dorothy Vaneman went upstairs to dress. Mrs. Vaneman's eyes followed her daughter's tall, trim figure more than a little apprehensively. She was wondering about this engagement. True, Richard was a fine chap and might make a name for himself, but at present he was a nobody and, socially, he would always be a nobody . . . and men of wealth, of distinction, of impeccable social status, had paid court . . . but Dorothy—no, "stubborn" was not too strong a term—when Dorothy made up her mind . . .

Unaware of her mother's look, Dorothy went happily up the stairs. She glanced at the clock, saw that it was only a little after six, and sat down at her dressing table, upon which there stood a picture of Richard. A strong, not unhandsome face, with keen, wide-set gray eyes; the wide brow of the thinker, surmounted by thick, unruly, dark hair; the firm, square jaw of the born fighter—such was the man whose vivid personality, fierce impetuosity, and indomitable perseverance had set him apart from all other men ever since their first meeting, and who had rapidly cleared the field of all other aspirants for her favor. Her breath came faster and her cheeks showed a lovelier color as she sat there, the lights playing in her heavy auburn hair and a tender smile upon her lips.

Dorothy dressed with unusual care and, the last touches deftly made, went downstairs and out upon the porch to wait for her guest.

Half an hour passed. Mrs. Vaneman came to the door and said anxiously, "I wonder if anything could have happened to him?"

"Of course there hasn't." Dorothy tried to keep all concern out of her voice. "Traffic jams—or perhaps he has been picked up again for speeding. Can Alice keep dinner a little longer?"

"To be sure," her mother answered, and disappeared.

But when another half hour had passed Dorothy went in, holding her head somewhat higher than usual and wearing a say-something-if-you-dare expression.

The meal was eaten in polite disregard of the unused plate. The family left the table. For Dorothy the evening was endless; but at the usual time it was ten o'clock, and then ten-thirty, and then Seaton appeared.

Dorothy opened the door, but Seaton did not come in. He stood close to her, but did not touch her. His eyes searched her face anxiously. Upon his face was a look of indecision, almost of fright—a look so foreign to his usual expression that the girl smiled in spite of herself.

"I'm awfully sorry, sweetheart, but I couldn't help it. You've got a right to be sore and I ought to be kicked from here to there, but are you too sore to let me talk to you for a couple of minutes?"

"I was never so mad at anybody in my life, until I started getting scared witless. I simply couldn't and can't believe you'd do anything like that on purpose. Come in."

He came. She closed the door. He half-extended his arms, then paused, irresolute, like a puppy hoping for a pat but expecting a kick. She grinned then, and came into his arms.

"But what *happened*, Dick?" she asked later. "Something terrible, to make you act like this. I've never seen you act so—so funny."

"Not terrible, Dotty, just extraordinary. So outrageously extraordinary that before I begin I wish you'd look me in the eye and tell me if you have any doubts about my sanity."

She led him into the living room, held his face up to the light, and made a pretense of studying his eyes.

"Richard Ballinger Seaton, I certify that you are entirely sane—quite the sanest man I ever knew. Now tell me the worst. Did you blow up the Bureau with a C-bomb?"

"Nothing like that," he laughed. "Just a thing I can't understand. You know I've been reworking the platinum wastes that have been accumulating for the last ten or fifteen years."

"Yes, you told me you'd recovered a small fortune in platinum and some of those other metals. You thought you'd found a brand-new one. Did you?"

"I sure did. After I'd separated out everything I could identify, there was quite a lot of something left—something that didn't respond to any tests I knew or could find in the literature.

"That brings us up to today. As a last resort, because there wasn't anything else left, I started testing for trans-uranics, and there it was. A stable—almost stable, I mean—isotope; up where no almost-stable isotopes are supposed to exist. Up where I would've bet my last shirt no such isotope could possibly exist.

"Well, I was trying to electrolyze it out when the fireworks started. The solution started to fizz over, so I grabbed the beaker—fast. The wires dropped onto the steam-bath and the whole outfit, except the beaker, took off out of the window at six or eight times the speed of sound and in a straight line, without dropping a foot in as far as I could keep it in sight with a pair of good binoculars. And my hunch is that it's still going. That's what happened. It's enough to knock any physicist into an outside loop, and with my one-cylinder brain I got to thinking about it and simply didn't come to until after ten o'clock. All I can say is, I'm sorry and I love you. As much as I ever did or could. More, if possible. And I always will. Can you let it go—this time?"

"Dick . . . oh, Dick!"

There was more—much more—but eventually Seaton mounted his motorcycle and Dorothy walked beside him down to the street. A final kiss and the man drove away.

After the last faint glimmer of red tail-light had disappeared in the darkness Dorothy made her way to her room, breathing a long and slightly tremulous, but supremely happy sigh.

chapter 3

SEATON'S CHILDHOOD HAD BEEN SPENT IN the mountains of northern Idaho, a region not much out of the pioneer stage and offering few inducements to intellectual effort. He could only dimly remember his mother, a sweet, gentle woman with a great love for books; but his father, "Big Fred" Seaton, a man of but one love, almost filled the vacant place. Fred owned a quarter-section of virgin white-pine timber, and in that splendid grove he established a home for himself and his motherless boy.

In front of the cabin lay a level strip of meadow, beyond which rose a magnificent, snow-crowned peak that caught the earliest rays of the sun.

This mountain, dominating the entire countryside, was to the boy a challenge, a question, and a secret. He accepted the challenge, scaling its steep sides, hunting its forests, and fishing its streams. He toughened his sturdy young body by days and nights upon its slopes. He puzzled over the question of its origin as he lay upon the needles under some monster pine. He put staggering questions to his father; and when in books he found some partial answers his joy was complete. He discovered some of the mountain's secrets then—some of the laws that govern the world of matter, some of the beginnings man's mind has made toward understanding the hidden mechanism of Nature's great simplicity.

Each taste of knowledge whetted his appetite for more. Books! Books! More and more he devoured them; finding in them meat for the hunger that filled him, answers to the questions that haunted him.

After Big Fred lost his life in the forest fire that destroyed his property, Seaton turned his back upon the woods forever. He worked his way through high school and won a scholarship at college. Study was a pleasure to his keen mind; and he had ample time for athletics, for which his backwoods life had fitted him outstandingly. He went out for everything, and excelled in football and tennis.

In spite of the fact that he had to work his way he was popular with his college mates, and his popularity was not lessened by an almost professional knowledge of sleight-of-hand. His long, strong fingers could move faster than the eye could follow, and many a lively college party watched in vain to see how he did what he did.

After graduating with highest honors as a physical chemist, he was appointed research fellow in a great university, where he won his Ph.D. by brilliant research upon rare metals—his dissertation having the lively title of "Some Observations upon Certain Properties of Certain Metals, Including Certain Trans-Uranic Elements." Soon afterward he had his own room in the Rare Metals Laboratory, in Washington, D.C.

He was a striking figure—well over six feet in height, broad-shouldered, narrow-waisted, a man of tremendous physical strength. He did not let himself grow soft in his laboratory job, but kept in hard, fine condition. He spent most of his spare time playing tennis, swimming and motor-cycling.

As a tennis-player he quickly became well known in Washington sporting and social circles. During the District Tournament he met M. Reynolds Crane—known to only a very few intimates as "Martin"—the multi-millionaire explorer-archaeologist-sportsman who was then District singles champion. Seaton had cleared the lower half of the list and played Crane in the final round. Crane succeeded in retaining his title, but only after five of the most grueling, most bitterly contested sets ever seen in Washington.

Impressed by Seaton's powerful, slashing game, Crane suggested that they train together as a doubles team. Seaton accepted instantly, and the combination was highly effective.

Practising together almost daily, each came to know the other as a man of his own kind, and a real friendship grew up between them. When the Crane-Seaton team had won the District Championship and had gone to the semi-finals of the National before losing, the two were upon a footing which most brothers could have envied. Their friendship was such that neither Crane's immense wealth and high social standing nor Seaton's comparative poverty and lack of standing offered any obstacle whatever. Their comradeship was the same, whether they were in Seaton's modest room or in Crane's palatial yacht.

Crane had never known the lack of anything that money could buy. He had inherited his fortune and had little or nothing to do with its management, preferring to delegate that job to financial specialists. However, he was in no sense an idle rich man with no purpose in life. As well as being an explorer and an archaeologist and a sportsman, he was also an engineer—a good one—and a rocket-instrument man second to none in the world.

The old Crane estate in Chevy Chase was now, of course, Martin's, and he had left it pretty much as it was. He had, however, altered one room, the library, and it was now peculiarly typical of the man. It was a large room, very long, with many windows. At one end was a huge fireplace, before which Crane often sat with his long legs outstretched, studying one or several books from the cases close at hand. The essential furnishings were of a rigid simplicity, but the treasures he had gathered transformed the room into a veritable museum.

He played no instrument, but in a corner stood a magnificent piano, bare of any ornament; and a Stradivarius reposed in a special cabinet. Few people were asked to play either of those instruments; but to those few Crane listened in silence, and his brief words of thanks showed his real appreciation of music.

He made few friends, not because he hoarded his friendship, but because, even more than most rich men, he had been forced to erect around his real self an almost impenetrable screen.

As for women, Crane frankly avoided them, partly because his greatest interests in life were things in which women had neither interest nor place, but mostly because he had for years been the prime target of the man-hunting debutantes and the matchmaking mothers of three continents.

Dorothy Vaneman with whom he had become acquainted through his friendship with Seaton, had been admitted to his friendship. Her frank comradeship was a continuing revelation, and it was she who had last played for him.

She and Seaton had been caught near his home by a sudden shower and had dashed in for shelter. While the rain beat outside, Crane had suggested that she pass the time by playing his "fiddle." Dorothy, a Doctor of Music and an accomplished violinist, realized with the first sweep of the bow that she was playing an instrument such as she had known only in her dreams, and promptly forgot everything else. She forgot the rain, the listeners, the time and the place; she simply poured into that wonderful violin everything she had of beauty, of tenderness, of artistry.

Sure, true, and full the tones filled the big room, and in Crane's vision there rose a home filled with happy work, with laughter and companionship. Sensing the girl's dreams as the music filled his ears, he realized as never before in his busy and purposeful life what a home with the right woman could be like. No thought of love for Dorothy entered his mind—he knew that the love existing between her and Dick was of the sort that only death could alter—but he knew that she had unwittingly given him a great gift. Often thereafter in his lonely hours he saw that dream home, and knew that nothing less than its realization would ever satisfy him.

chapter **4**

RETURNING TO HIS BOARDING HOUSE, SEATON undressed and went to bed, but not to sleep. He knew that he had seen what could very well become a workable space-drive that afternoon. . . . After an hour of trying to force himself to sleep he gave up, went to his desk, and started to study. The more he studied, the more strongly convinced he became that this first thought was right—the thing *could* become a space-drive.

By breakfast time he had the beginnings of a tentative theory roughed out, and also had gained some idea of the nature and magnitude of the obstacles to overcome.

Arriving at the Laboratory, he found that Scott had spread the news of his adventure, and his room was soon the center of interest. He described what he had seen and done to the impromptu assembly of scientists, and was starting in on the explanation he had deduced when he was interrupted by Ferdinand Scott.

"Quick, Dr. Watson, the needle!" he exclaimed. Seizing a huge pipette from a rack, he went through the motions of injecting its contents into Seaton's arm.

"It does sound like a combination of science-fiction and Sherlock Holmes," one of the visitors remarked.

" 'Nobody Holme,' you mean," Scott said, and a general chorus of friendly but skeptical jibes followed.

"Wait a minute, you hidebound dopes, and I'll show you!" Seaton snapped. He dipped a short piece of copper wire into his solution.

It did not turn brown; and when he touched it with his conductors, nothing happened. The group melted away. As they left, some of the men maintained a pitying silence, but

Seaton heard one half-smothered chuckle and several remarks about "cracking under the strain."

Bitterly humiliated at the failure of his demonstration, Seaton scowled morosely at the offending wire. Why should the thing work twice yesterday and not even once today? He reviewed his theory and could find no flaw in it. There *must* have been something going last night that wasn't going now . . . something capable of affecting ultra-fine structure. . . . It had to be either in the room or very close by . . . and no ordinary generator or X-ray machine could possibly have had any effect. . . .

There was one possibility—only one. The machine in DuQuesne's room next to his own, the machine he himself had, every once in a while, helped rebuild.

It was not a cyclotron, not a betatron. In fact, it had as yet no official name. Unofficially, it was the "whatsitron," or the "maybetron," or the "itaintsotron" or any one of many less descriptive and more profane titles which he, DuQuesne, and the other researchers used among themselves. It did not take up much room. It did not weigh ten thousand tons. It did not require a million kilowatts of power. Nevertheless it was—theoretically—capable of affecting super-fine structure.

But in the next room? Seaton doubted it.

However, there was nothing else, and it *had* been running the night before—its glare was unique and unmistakable. Knowing that DuQuesne would turn his machine on very shortly, Seaton sat in suspense, staring at the wire. Suddenly the subdued reflection of the familiar glare appeared on the wall outside his door—and simultaneously the treated wire turned brown.

Heaving a profound sigh of relief, Seaton again touched the bit of metal with the wires from the Redeker cell. It disappeared instantaneously with a high whining sound.

Seaton started for the door, to call his neighbors in for another demonstration, but in mid-stride changed his mind. He wouldn't tell anybody anything until he knew something about the thing himself. He had to find out what it was, what it did, how and why it did it, and how—or if—it could be controlled. That meant time, apparatus and, above all, money. Money meant Crane; and Mart would be interested, anyway.

Seaton made out a leave-slip for the rest of the day, and was soon piloting his motorcycle out Connecticut Avenue and into Crane's private drive. Swinging under the imposing porte-cochère he jammed on his brakes and stopped in a shower of gravel, a perilous two inches from granite. He dashed up the steps and held his finger firmly against the bell button. The door was opened hastily by Crane's Japanese servant, whose face lit up on seeing the visitor.

"Hello, Shiro. Is the honorable son of Heaven up yet?"

"Yes, sir, but he is at present in his bath."

"Tell him to snap it up, please. Tell him I've got a thing on the fire that'll break him right off at the ankles."

Bowing the guest to a chair in the library, Shiro hurried away. Returning shortly, he placed before Seaton the *Post*, the *Herald*, and a jar of Seaton's favorite brand of tobacco, and said, with his unfailing bow, "Mr. Crane will appear in less than one moment, sir."

Seaton filled and lit his briar and paced up and down the room, smoking furiously. In a short time Crane came in.

"Good morning, Dick." The men shook hands cordially. "Your message was slightly garbled in transmission. Something about a fire and ankles is all that came through. What fire? And whose ankles were—or are about to be—broken?"

Seaton repeated.

"Ah, yes, I thought it must have been something like that. While I have breakfast, will you have lunch?"

"Thanks, Mart, guess I will. I was too excited to eat much of anything this morning." A table appeared and the two men sat down at it. "I'll just spring it on you cold, I guess. Just what would you think of working with me on a widget to liberate and control the entire constituent energy of metallic copper? Not in little dribbles and drabbles, like fission or fusion, but one hundred point zero zero zero zero per cent conversion? No radiation, no residue, no by-products—which means no shielding or protection would be necessary—just pure and total conversion of matter to controllable energy?"

Crane, who had a cup of coffee half-way to his mouth, stopped it in mid-air, and stared at Seaton eye to eye. This, in Crane the Imperturbable, betrayed more excitement than Seaton had ever seen him show. He finished lifting the cup, sipped, and replaced the cup studiously, meticulously, in the exact center of its saucer.

"That would undoubtedly constitute the greatest technological advance the world has ever seen," he said, finally. "But, if you will excuse the question, how much of that is fact, and how much fancy? That is, what portion have you actually done, and what portion is more or less justified projection into the future?"

"About one to ninety-nine—maybe less," Seaton admitted. "I've hardly started. I don't blame you for gagging on it a bit—everybody down at the lab thinks I'm nuttier than a fruitcake. Here's what actually happened," and he described the accident in full detail. "And here's the theory I've worked out, so far, to cover it." He went on to explain.

"That's the works," Seaton concluded, tensely, "as clearly as I can put it. What do you think of it?"

"An extraordinary story, Dick . . . really extraordinary. I understand why the men at the Laboratory thought as they did, especially after your demonstration failed. I would like to see it work, myself, before discussing further actions or procedures."

"Fine! That suits me down to the ground—get into your clothes and I'll take you down to the lab on my bike. If I don't show you enough to make your eyes stick out a foot I'll eat that motorsickle, clear down to the tires!"

As soon as they arrived at the Laboratory, Seaton assured himself that the "whatsitron" was still running, and arranged his demonstration. Crane remained silent, but watched closely every movement Seaton made.

"I take a piece of ordinary copper wire, so," Seaton began. "I dip it into this beaker of solution, thus. Note the marked change in its appearance. I place the wire upon this bench —so—with the treated end pointing out of the window. . . ."

"No. Toward the wall. I want to see the hole made."

"Very well—with the treated end pointing toward that brick wall. This is an ordinary eight-watt Redeker cell. When I touch these lead-wires to the treated wire, watch closely. The speed is supersonic, but you'll hear it, whether you see what happens or not. Ready?"

"Ready." Crane riveted his gaze upon the wire.

Seaton touched the wire with the Redeker leads, and it promptly and enthusiastically disappeared. Turning to Crane, who was staring alternately at the new hole in the wall and at the spot where the wire had been, he cried exultantly, "Well, Doubting Thomas, how do you like *them* potatoes? Did that wire travel, or did it not? Was there some kick to it, or was there not?"

Crane walked to the wall and examined the hole minutely. He explored it with his forefinger; then, bending over, looked through it.

"Hm-m-m . . . well . . ." he said, straightening up. "That hole is as real as the bricks of the wall . . . . . and you certainly did not make it by sleight-of-hand . . . if you can control

that power . . . put it into a hull . . . harness it to the wheels
of industry . . . You are offering me a partnership?"

"Yes. I can't even afford to quit the Service, to say nothing
of setting up what we'll have to have for this job. Besides,
working this out is going to be a lot more than a one-man
job. It'll take all the brains both of us have got, and probably
a nickle's worth besides, to lick it."

"Check. I accept—and thanks a lot for letting me in."
The two shook hands vigorously. Crane said, "The first thing
to do, and it must be done with all possible speed, is to get
unassailably clear title to that solution, which is, of course,
government property. How do you propose going about that?"

"It's government property—technically—yes; but it was
worthless after I had recovered the values and ordinarily it
would have been poured down the sink. I saved it just to
satisfy my own curiosity as to what was in it. I'll just stick
it in a paper bag and walk out with it, and if anybody asks
any questions later, it simply went down the drain, as it
was supposed to."

"Not good enough. We must have clear title, signed,
sealed, and delivered. Can it be done?"

"I think so . . . pretty sure of it. There'll be an auction in
about an hour—they have one every Friday—and I can get
this bottle of waste condemned easy enough. I can't imagine
anybody bidding on it but us. I'll fly at it."

"One other thing first. Will there be any difficulty about
your resignation?"

"Not a chance." Seaton grinned mirthlessly. "They all
think I'm screwy—they'll be glad to get rid of me so easy."

"All right. Go ahead—the solution first."

"Check," Seaton said; and very shortly the bottle, sealed
by the chief clerk and labeled *Item QX47R769BC: one bottle
containing waste solution*, was on its way to the auction room.

Nor was there any more difficulty about his resignation
from the Rare Metals Laboratory. Gossip spreads rapidly.

When the auctioneer reached the one-bottle lot, he looked
at it in disgust. Why auction one bottle, when he had been
selling barrels of them? But it had an official number; auc-
tioned it must be.

"One bottle full of waste," he droned, tonelessly. "Any
bidders? If not, I'll throw it—"

Seaton jumped forward and opened his mouth to yell, but
was quelled by a sharp dig in the ribs.

"Five cents." He heard Crane's calm voice.

"Five cents bid. Any more? Going—going—"

Seaton gulped to steady his voice. "Ten cents."

"Ten cents. Any more? Going—going—gone," and Item QX47R769BC became the officially-recorded personal property of Richard B. Seaton.

Just as the transfer was completed Scott caught of Seaton.

"Hello, Nobody Holme!" he called gaily. "Was that the famous solution of zero? Wish we'd known it—we'd've had fun bidding you up."

"Not too much, Ferdy." Seaton was calm enough, now that the precious solution was definitely his own. "This is a cash sale, you know, so it wouldn't have cost us much, anyway."

"That's true, too," Scott admitted, nonchalantly enough. "This poor government clerk is broke, as usual. But who's the 'we'?"

"Mr. Scott, meet my friend M. Reynolds Crane," and, as Scott's eyes opened in astonishment, he added, "He doesn't think I'm ready for St. Elizabeth's yet."

"It's the bunk, Mr. Crane," Scott said, twirling his right forefinger near his right ear. "Dick used to be a good old wagon, but he done broke down."

"That's what you think!" Seaton took a half step forward, but checked himself even before Crane touched his elbow. "Wait a few weeks, Scotty, and see."

The two took a cab back to Crane's house—the bottle being far too valuable to risk on any motorcycle—where Crane poured out a little of the solution into a small vial, which he placed in his safe. He then put the large bottle, carefully packed, into his massive underground vault, remarking, "We'll take no chances at all with that."

"Right," Seaton agreed. "Well, let's get busy. The first thing to do is to hunt up a small laboratory that's for rent."

"Wrong. The organization of our company comes first— suppose I should die before we solve the problem? I suggest something like this. Neither of us want to handle the company as such, so it will be a stock company, capitalized at one million dollars, with ten thousand shares of stock. McQueen, who is handling my affairs at the bank, can be president; Winters, his attorney, and Robinson, his C.P.A., secretary and treasurer; you and I will be superintendent and general manager. To make up seven directors, we could elect Mr. Vaneman and Shiro. As for the capital, I will put in half a million; you will put in your idea and your solution, at a preliminary, tentative valuation of half a million—"

"But, Mart—"

"Hold on, Dick. Let me finish. They are worth much more than that, of course, and will be revalued later, but that will do for a start. . . ."

"Hold on yourself for a minute. Why tie up all that cash when a few thousand bucks is all we'll need?"

"A few thousand? Think a minute, Dick. How much testing equipment will you need? How about salaries and wages? How much of a spaceship can you build for a million dollars? And power-plants run from a hundred million up. Convinced?"

"Well, maybe . . . except, right at first, I thought . . ."

"You will see that this is a very small start, the way it is. Now to call the meeting."

He called McQueen, the president of the great trust company in whose care the bulk of his fortune was. Seaton, listening to the brief conversation, realized as never before what power was wielded by his friend.

In a surprisingly short time the men were assembled in Crane's library. Crane called the meeting to order; outlined the nature and scope of the proposed corporation; and The Seaton-Crane Company, Engineers, began to come into being.

After the visitors had gone, Seaton asked, "Do you know what kind of a rental agent to call to get hold of a laboratory?"

"For a while at least, the best place for you to work is right here."

"Here! You don't want stuff like that loose around here, do you?"

"Yes. The reasons are: first, privacy; second, convenience. We have much of the material and equipment you will need already on hand, out in the hangar and the shops, and plenty of room to install anything new you may need. Third, no curiosity. The Cranes have been inventors, tinkerers, and mechanics so long, that no planning board has ever been able to zone our shops out; and our nearest neighbors—and none are very near, as you know, since I own over forty acres here—are so used to peculiar happenings that they no longer pay any attention to anything that goes on here."

"Fine! If that's the way you want it, it suits me down to the ground. Let's get busy!"

chapter 5

DR. MARC C. DUQUESNE WAS A TALL, POW-
erful man, built very much like Richard Seaton. His thick,
slightly wavy hair was intensely black. His eyes, only a trifle
lighter in shade, were surmounted by thick black eyebrows,
which grew together above his aquiline, finely-chiseled nose.
His face, although not pale, appeared so because of the heavy
black beard always showing through, even after the closest
possible shave. In his early thirties, he was widely known as
one of the best men in his field.

Scott came into his laboratory immediately after the auction, finding him leaning over the console of the whatsitron,
his forbidding but handsome face strangely illuminated by
the greenish-yellowish-blue glare of the machine.

"Hello, Blackie," Scott said. "What d'you think of Seaton?
Think he's quite right in the head?"

"Speaking off-hand," DuQuesne replied, without looking
up, "I'd say he's been putting in too many hours working and
not enough sleeping. I don't think he's insane—I'd swear in
court that he's the sanest crazy man I ever heard of."

"I think he's a plain nut, myself—that was a lulu he pulled
yesterday. He seems to believe it himself, though. He got
them to put that junk solution into the auction this noon
and he and M. Reynolds Crane bid it in for ten cents."

"M. Reynolds Crane?" DuQuesne managed to conceal his
start of surprise. "Where does he come in on this?"

"Oh, he and Seaton have been buddy-buddy for a long
time, you know. Probably humoring him. After they got the
solution they called a cab and somebody said the address they
gave the hackie was Crane's, the other side Chevy Chase,
but . . . oh, that's my call—so long."

As Scott left, DuQuesne strode over to his desk, a new
expression, half of chagrin, half of admiration, on his face.
He picked up his telephone and dialed a number.

"Brookings? DuQuesne speaking. I've got to see you as
fast as I can get there. Can't talk on the phone. . . . Yes,
I'll be right out."

He left the Laboratory building and was soon in the private

office of the head of the Washington, or "diplomatic," branch of the immense World Steel Corporation.

"How do you do, Dr. DuQuesne," Brookings said, as he seated his visitor. "You seem excited."

"Not excited, but in a hurry. The biggest thing in history is just breaking and we've got to work fast if we want to land it. But before I start—have you any sneaking doubts that I know what I'm talking about?"

"Why, no, doctor, not the slightest. You are widely known; you have helped us in various de—in various matters."

"Say it, Brookings. 'Deals' is right. This is going to be the biggest ever. It should be easy—one simple killing and an equally simple burglary—and won't mean wholesale murder, like that tungsten job."

"Oh, no, doctor, not murder. Accidents."

"I call things by their right names. I'm not squeamish. But what I'm here about is that Seaton, of our division, has discovered, more or less accidentally, total conversion atomic energy."

"And that means?"

"To break it down to where you can understand it, it means a billion kilowatts per plant at a total amortized cost of approximately one one-hundredth of a mil per KW hour."

"Huh?" A look of scornful disbelief settled on Brookings' face.

"Sneer if you like. Your ignorance doesn't change the facts and doesn't hurt my feelings a bit. Call Chambers in and ask him what would happen if a man should liberate the total energy of a hundred pounds of cooper in, say, ten microseconds."

"Pardon me, doctor. I didn't mean to insult you. I'll call him in."

Brookings called, and a man in white appeared. In response to the question he thought for a moment, then smiled.

"At a rough guess, it would blow the whole world into vapor and might blow it clear out of its orbit. However, you needn't worry about anything like that happening, Mr. Brookings. It won't. It can't."

"Why not?"

"Because only two nuclear reactions yield energy—fission and fusion. Very heavy elements fission; very light elements fuse; intermediate ones, such as copper, do neither. Any possible operation on the copper atom, such as splitting, must necessarily absorb vastly more energy than it produces. Is that all?"

"That's all. Thanks."

"You see?" Brookings said, when they were again alone, "Chambers is a good man, too, and he says it's impossible."

"As far as he knows, he's right. I'd have said the same thing this morning. However, it has just been done."

"How?"

DuQuesne repeated certain parts of Seaton's story.

"But suppose the man is crazy? He could be, couldn't he?"

"Yeah, he's crazy—like a fox. If it were only Seaton, I might buy that; but nobody ever thought M. Reynolds Crane had any loose screws. With *him* backing Seaton you can bet your last dollar that Seaton showed him plenty of real stuff." As a look of conviction appeared upon Brookings' face DuQuesne went on. "Don't you understand? The solution was government property and he had to do something to make everybody think it was worthless, so he could get title to it. It was a bold move—it would have been foolhardy in anyone else. The reason he got away with it is that he's always been an open-faced talker, always telling everything he knows. He fooled me completely, and I'm not usually asleep out of bed."

"What is your idea? Where do we come in?"

"You come in by getting that solution away from Seaton and Crane, and furnishing the money to develop the stuff and to build, under my direction, such a power plant as the world never saw before."

"Why is it necessary to get that particular solution? Why not refine some more platinum wastes?"

"Not a chance. Chemists have been recovering platinum for a hundred years, and nothing like that was ever found before. The stuff, whatever it is, must have been present in some particular lot of platinum. They haven't got all of it there is in the world, of course, but the chance of finding any without knowing exactly what to look for is extremely slight. Besides, we *must* have a monopoly on it—Crane would be satisfied with ten per cent net profit. No, we've got to get every milliliter of that solution and we've got to kill Seaton— he knows too much. I want to take a couple of your goons and attend to it tonight."

Brookings thought for a minute, his face blandly empty of expression. Then he spoke.

"I'm sorry, doctor, but we can't do it. It's too flagrant, too risky. Besides, we can afford to buy it from Seaton if, as, and when he proves it is worth anything."

"Bah!" DuQuesne snorted. "Who do you think you're kidding? Do you think I told you enough so that you can sidetrack me out of the deal? Get that idea out of your head—fast. There are only two men in the world who can handle it—R. B. Seaton and M. C. DuQuesne. Take your pick. Put anybody else on it—anybody else—and he'll blow himself and his whole neighborhood out beyond the orbit of Mars."

Brookings, caught flat-footed and half convinced of the truth of DuQuesne's statements, still temporized.

"You're very modest, DuQuesne."

"Modesty gets a man praise, but I prefer cash. However, you ought to know by this time that what I say is true. And I'm in a hurry. The difficulty of getting hold of that solution is growing greater every minute and my price is rising every minute."

"What is your price at the present minute?"

"Ten thousand dollars a month during development, five million cash when the first plant goes onto the line, and ten per cent of the net—on all plants—thereafter."

"Oh, come, doctor, let's be sensible. You don't mean that."

"I don't say anything I don't mean. I've done a lot of dirty work for you people and never got much of anything out of it—I couldn't force you without exposing myself. But this time I've got you where the hair's short and I'm going to collect. And you still can't kill me—I'm not Ainsworth. Not only because you'll have to have me, but because it'd still send all you big shots clear down to Perkins, to the chair, or up the river for life."

"Please, DuQuesne, please don't use such language!"

"Why not?" DuQuesne's voice was cold and level. "What do a few lives amount to, as long as they're not yours or mine? I can trust you, more or less, and you can trust me the same, because you know I can't send you up without going with you. If that's the way you want it, I'll let you try it without me—you won't get far. So decide, right now, whether you want me now, or later. If it's later, the first two of those figures I gave you will be doubled."

"We can't do business on any such terms." Brookings shook his head. "We can buy the power rights from Seaton for less."

"You want it the hard way, eh?" DuQuesne sneered as he came to his feet. "Go ahead. Steal the solution. But don't give your man much of it, not more than half a teaspoonful —I want as much as possible of it left. Set up the laboratory a hundred miles from anywhere—not that I give a damn how many people you kill, but I don't want to go along—and caution whoever does the work to use very small quantities of copper. Good-bye."

As the door closed behind the cynical scientist, Brookings took a small instrument, very like a watch, from his pocket, touched a button, raised it to his lips, and spoke. "Perkins."

"Yes, sir."

"M. Reynolds Crane has in or around his house somewhere a small bottle of solution."

"Yes, sir. Can you describe it?"

"Not exactly." Brookings went on to tell his minion all he knew about the matter. "If the bottle were only partly emptied and filled up with water, I don't believe anybody would notice the difference."

"Probably not, sir. Good-bye."

Brookings then took his personal typewriter out of a drawer and typed busily for a few minutes. Among other things, he wrote:

". . . and do not work on too much copper at once. I gather that an ounce or two should be enough. . . ."

chapter **6**

FROM DAYLIGHT UNTIL LATE IN THE EVENing Seaton worked in the shop, sometimes supervising expert mechanics, sometimes working alone. Every night when Crane went to bed he saw Seaton in his room in a cloud of smoke, poring over blueprints or seated at the computer, making interminable calculations. Deaf to Crane's remonstrances, he was driving himself at an unhuman rate, completely absorbed in his project. While he did not forget Dorothy, he had a terrific lot to do and none of it was getting done. He was going to see her just as soon as he was over this hump, he insisted; but every hump was followed by another, higher and worse. And day after day went by.

Meanwhile, Dorothy was feeling considerably glum. Here was her engagement only a week old—and what an engagement! Before that enchanted evening he had been an almost daily visitor. They had ridden and talked and played together, and he had forced his impetuous way into all her plans. Now, after she had promised to marry him, he had called once—at eleven o'clock!—with his mind completely out of this world, and she hadn't even heard from him for six long days. A queer happening at the laboratory seemed scant excuse for such long-continued neglect, and she knew no other.

Puzzled and hurt, her mother's solicitous looks unbearable, she left the house for a long, aimless walk. She paid no attention to the spring beauty around her. She did not even notice footsteps following her, and was too deeply engrossed in her own somber thoughts to be more than mildly suprised when Martin Crane spoke to her. For a while she tried to rouse herself into animation, but her usual ease had deserted her and her false gaiety did not deceive the keen-minded Crane. Soon they were walking along together in silence, a silence finally broken by the man.

"I have just left Seaton," he said. Paying no attention to her startled glance, he went on, "Did you ever see anyone else with his singleness of purpose? Of course, though, that is one of the traits that make him what he is. . . . He is working himself into a breakdown. Has he told you about leaving the Rare Metals Laboratory?"

"No, I haven't seen him since the night the accident, or discovery, or whatever it was, happened. He tried to explain it to me then, but what little I could understand of what he said sounded simply preposterous."

"I can't explain the thing to you—Dick himself can't explain it to me—but I can give you an idea of what we both think it may come to."

"I wish you would. I'll be mighty glad to hear it."

"Dick discovered something that converts copper into pure energy. That water-bath took off in a straight line—"

"That *still* sounds preposterous, Martin," the girl interrupted, "even when you say it."

"Careful, Dorothy," he cautioned her. "Nothing that actually happens is or can be preposterous. But as I said, this copper bath left Washington in a straight line for scenes unknown. We intend to follow it in a suitable vehicle."

He paused, looking at his companion's face. She did not speak, and he went on in his matter-of-fact tone.

"Building the spaceship is where I come in. As you know, I have almost as much money as Dick has brains; and some day, before the summer is over, we expect to go somewhere . . . some place a considerable distance from this earth."

Then, after enjoining strict secrecy, he told her what he had seen in the laboratory and described the present state of affairs.

"But if he thought of all that . . . was brilliant enough to work out such a theory and to actually plan such an unheard-of thing as space-travel . . . all on such a slight foundation of fact . . . why couldn't he have *told* me?"

"He fully intended to. He still intends to. Don't believe for a moment that his absorption implies any lack of love for you. I was coming to visit you about that when I saw you out here. He's driving himself unmercifully. He eats hardly anything and doesn't seem to sleep at all. He has to take it easy or break down, but nothing I can say has had any effect. Can you think of anything you, or you and I together, can do?"

Dorothy still walked along, but it was a different Dorothy. She was erect and springy, her eyes sparkled, all her charm and vitality were back in force.

"I'll say I can!" she breathed. "I'll stuff him to the ears and put him to sleep right after dinner, the big dope!"

This time it was Crane who was surprised, so surprised that he stopped, practically in mid-stride. "How?" he demanded. "You talk about something being preposterous—how?"

"Maybe you hadn't better know the gory details." She grinned impishly. "You lack quite a bit, Marty, of being the world's best actor, and Dick mustn't be warned. Just run along home, and be sure you're there when I get there. I've got to do some phoning. . . . I'll be there at six o'clock, and tell Shiro not to make you two any dinner."

She was there at six o'clock.

"Where is he, Marty? Out in the shop?"

"Yes."

In the shop, she strode purposefully toward Seaton's oblivious back. "Hi, Dick. How's it coming?"

"Huh?" He started violently, almost jumping off his stool—then did jump off it as the knowledge filtered through that it was really Dorothy who was standing at his back. He swept her off her feet in the intensity of his embrace; she pressed her every inch tighter and tighter against his rock-hard body. Their lips met and clung.

Dorothy finally released herself enough to look into his eyes. "I was so mad, Dick. I simply didn't know whether to kiss you or kill you, but I decided to kiss you—this time."

"I know, sweetheart. I've been trying my level best to get a couple of hours to come over and see you, but everything's been going so slow—my head's so thick it takes a thousand years for an idea to percolate—"

"Hush! I've been doing a lot of thinking this last week, especially today. I love you as you are. I can either do that or give you up. I can't even imagine giving you up, because I know I'd cold-bloodedly strangle with her own hair any woman who ever cocked an eye at you. . . . Come on, Dick, no more work tonight. I'm taking you and Martin home for dinner." Then, as his eyes strayed involuntarily back toward the computer, she said, more forcefully, "I—said—no—more—work—tonight. Do you want to fight about it?"

"Uh-uh! I'll say I don't—I wasn't even *thinking* of working!" Seaton was panic-stricken. "No fights, Dottie. Not with you. Ever. About anything. Believe me."

"I do, lover," and, arms around each other, they strolled unhurriedly up to and into the house.

Crane accepted enthusiastically—for him—the invitation to dinner, and was going to dress, but Dorothy would not have it.

"Strictly informal," she insisted. "Just as you are."

"I'll wash up, then, and be with you in a sec," Seaton said, and left the room. Dorothy turned to Crane.

"I've got a tremendous favor to ask of you, Martin. I drove the Cad—it's air-conditioned, you know—could you possibly bring your Stradivarius along? My best violin would do, I'm sure, but I'd rather have the heaviest artillery I can get."

"I see—at last." Crane's face lit up. "Certainly. Play it outdoors in the rain, if necessary. Masterful strategy, Dorothy—masterful."

"Well, one does what one can," Dorothy murmured in mock modesty. Then, as Seaton appeared, she said, "Let's go, boys. Dinner is served at seven-thirty sharp, and we're going to be there right on the chime."

As they sat down at the table Dorothy studied again the changes that six days had made in Seaton. His face was pale and thin, almost haggard. Lines had appeared at the corners of his eyes and around his mouth, and faint but unmistakable blue rings encircled his eyes.

"You've been going altogether too hard, Dick. You've got to cut down."

"Oh no, I'm all right. I never felt better. I could whip a rattlesnake and give him the first bite!"

She laughed, but the look of concern did not leave her face.

During the meal no mention was made of the project, the conversation being deftly held to tennis, swimming, and other sports; and Seaton, whose plate was unobtrusively kept full, ate such a dinner as he had not eaten for weeks. After dessert they all went into the living room and ensconced themselves in comfortable chairs. The men smoked; all five continued their conversation.

After a time three left the room. Vaneman took Crane into his study to show him a rare folio; Mrs. Vaneman went upstairs, remarking plaintively that she *had* to finish writing that article, and if she put it off much longer she'd *never* get it done.

Dorothy said, "I skipped practice today, Dick, on account of traipsing out there after you two geniuses. Could you stand it to have me play at you for half an hour?"

"Don't fish, Dottie Dimple. You know there's nothing I'd like better. But if you want me to beg you I'll be glad to. Please—PUH-LEEZE—oh fair and musicianly damsel, fill ye circumambient atmosphere with thy tuneful notes."

"Wilco. Roger," she snickered. "Over and out."

She took up a violin—Crane's violin—and played. First his favorites: crashing selections from operas and solos by the great masters, abounding in harmonies on two strings. Then she slowly changed her playing to softer, simpler melodies, then to old, old songs. Seaton, listening with profound enjoyment, relaxed more and more. Pipe finished and hands at rest, his eyes closed of themselves and he lay back at ease. The music changed again, gradually, to reveries; each one softer, slower, dreamier than the last. Then to sheer, crooning lullabies; and it was in these that magnificent instrument and consumate artist combined to show their true qualities at their very best.

Dorothy diminuendoed the final note into silence and stood there, bow poised, ready to resume; but there was no need. Freed from the tyranny of the brain that had been driving it so unmercifully, Seaton's body had begun to make up for many hours of lost sleep.

Assured that he was really asleep, Dorothy tiptoed to the door of the study and whispered, "He's asleep in his chair."

"I believe that," her father smiled. "That last one was like a bottle of veronal—it was all Crane and I could do to keep each other awake. You're a smart girl."

"She is a musician," Crane said. "What a musician!"

"Partly me, of course, but—what a violin! But what'll we do with him? Let him sleep there?"

"No, he'd be more comfortable on the couch. I'll get a couple of blankets," Vaneman said.

He did so and the three went into the living room together. Seaton lay motionless, only the lifting and falling of his powerful chest showing that he was alive.

"You take his . . ."

"Sh . . Sh!" Dorothy whispered, intensely. "You'll wake him up, dad."

"Bosh! You couldn't wake him up now with a club. You take his head and shoulders, Crane—heave-ho!"

With Dorothy anxiously watching the proceedings and trying to help, the two men picked Seaton up out of the chair and carried him across the room to the couch. They removed his outer clothing; the girl arranged pillows and tucked blankets around him, then touched her lips lightly to his. "Good night, sweetheart," she whispered.

His lips responded faintly to her caress, and, ". . . dnigh . . ." he murmured in his sleep.

It was three o'clock in the afternoon when Seaton, looking vastly better, came into the shop. When Crane saw him and called out a greeting, he returned it with a sheepish grin.

"Don't say a word, Martin; I'm thinking it all, and then some. I never felt so cheap in my life as when I woke up on the Vanemans' couch this noon—where you helped put me, no doubt."

"No doubt at all," Crane agreed, cheerfully, "and listen to this. More of the same, or worse, if you keep on going as you were."

"Don't rub it in—can't you see I'm flat on my back with all four paws in the air? I'll be good. I'm going to bed at eleven every night and I'm going to see Dottie every other evening and all day Sunday."

"Very fine, if true—and it had better be true."

"It will, so help me. Well, while I was eating breakfast this morning—this afternoon, rather—I saw that missing factor in the theory. And don't tell me it was because I was rested up and fresh, either—I know it."

"I was refraining heroically from mentioning the fact."

"Thanks so much. Well, the knotty point, you remember, was what could be the possible effect of a small electric current in liberating the power. I think I've got it. It must shift the epsilon-gamma-zeta plane—and if it does, the rate of liberation must be zero when the angle theta is zero, and approach infinity as theta approaches pi over two."

"It does not," Crane contradicted, flatly. "It can't. The

orientation of that plane is fixed by temperature—by nothing
except temperature."

"That's so, usually, but that's where the X comes in. Here's
the proof. . . ."

On and on the argument raged. Reference works littered
the table and overflowed onto the floor, scratch-paper grew
into piles, both computers ran almost continuously.

Since the mathematical details of the Seaton-Crane Effect
are of little or no interest here, it will suffice to mention a
few of the conclusions at which the two men arrived. The
power could be controlled. It could drive—or pull—a spaceship. It could be used as an explosive, in violences ranging
from that of a twenty-millimeter shell up to any upper limit
desired, however fantastic when expressed in megatons of
T.N.T. There were many other possibilities inherent in their
final equations, possibilities which the men did not at that
time explore.

chapter 7

"SAY, BLACKIE," SCOTT CALLED FROM THE
door of DuQuesne's laboratory, "did you get the news flash
that just came over on KSKM-TV? It was right down your
alley."

"No. What about it?"

"Somebody piled up a million tons of tetryl, T.N.T., picric
acid, nitroglycerine, and so forth up in the hills and touched
it off. Blooie! Whole town of Bankerville, West Virginia—
population two hundred—gone. No survivors. No debris,
even, the man said. Just a hole in the ground a couple of
miles in diameter and God only knows how deep."

"Baloney!" DuQuesne snapped. "What would anybody be
doing with an atomic bomb up there?"

"That's the funny part of it—it wasn't an atomic bomb.
No radioactivity anywhere, not even a trace. Just skillions
and whillions of tons of high explosive and nobody can figure
it. 'All scientists baffled,' the flash said. How about you,
Blackie? You baffled, too?"

"I would be, if I believed any part of it." DuQuesne turned
back to his work.

"Well, don't blame *me* for it, I'm just telling you what Fritz Habelmann just said."

Since DuQuesne showed no interest at all in his news, Scott wandered away.

"The fool did it. That will cure him of sucking eggs—I hope," he muttered, and picked up his telephone.

"Operator? DuQuesne speaking. I am expecting a call here this afternoon. Please have the party call me at my home, Lincoln six four six two oh. . . . Thank you."

He left the building and got his car out of the parking lot. In less than half an hour he reached his house on Park Road, overlooking beautiful Rock Creek Park, in which he lived alone save for an elderly colored couple who were his servants.

In the busiest part of the afternoon Chambers rushed unannounced into Brookings' private office, his face white, a newspaper in his hand.

"Read that, Mr. Brookings!" he gasped.

Brookings read, his face turning gray. "Ours, of course."

"Ours," Chambers agreed, dully.

"The fool! Didn't you tell him to work with very small quantities?"

"I did. He said not to worry, he was taking no chances, he wouldn't have more than one gram of copper on hand at once in the whole laboratory."

"Well . . . I'll . . . be . . . jiggered!" Turning slowly to the telephone, Brookings called a number and asked for Doctor DuQuesne; then he called another.

"Brookings. I would like to see you as soon as possible. . . . I'll be there in about an hour. . . . Good-bye."

Brookings arrived and was shown into DuQuesne's study. The two shook hands perfunctorily and sat down. The scientist waited for the other to speak.

"You were right, doctor," Brookings said. "Our man couldn't handle it. I have contracts here. . . ."

"At twenty and ten?" DuQuesne's lips smiled, a cold, hard smile.

"Twenty and ten. The Company expects to pay for its mistakes. Here they are."

DuQuesne glanced over the documents and thrust them into a pocket. "I'll go over them with my attorney tonight and mail one copy back to you if he says to. In the meantime we may as well get started."

"What do you suggest?"

"First, the solution. You stole it, I—"

"Don't use such language, doctor!"

"Why not? I'm for direct action, first, last, and all the time. This thing is too important to mince words. Have you got it with you?"

"Yes. Here it is."

"Where's the rest of it?"

"All that we found is here, except for half a teaspoonful our expert had in his laboratory. We didn't get it all; only half of it. The rest was diluted with water, so it wouldn't be missed. We can get the rest of it later. That will cause a disturbance, but it may become. . . ."

"Half of it! You haven't a twentieth of it here. Seaton had about four hundred milliliters—almost a pint—of it. I wonder . . . who's holding out on—or double-crossing— whom?

"No, not you," he went on, as Brookings protested innocence. "That wouldn't make sense. Your thief turned in only this much. Could he be holding out on us . . . no, that doesn't make sense, either."

"No. You know Perkins."

"His crook missed the main bottle, then. That's where your methods give me an acute bellyache. When I want anything done I do it myself. But it isn't too late yet. I'll take a couple of your goons tonight and go out there."

"And do exactly what?"

"Shoot Seaton, open the safe, take their solution, plans, and notes. Loose cash, too, of course—I'll give that to the goons."

"No, no, doctor. That's too crude altogether. I could permit that only as the last possible resort."

"I say do it first. I'm afraid of pussyfooting and gum-shoeing around Seaton and Crane. Seaton has developed a lot of late, and Crane never was anybody's fool. They're a hard combination to beat, and we've done plenty worse and got away with it."

"Why not work it out from the solution we have, and then get the rest of it? Then, if Seaton had an accident, we could prove that we discovered the stuff long ago."

"Because development work on that stuff is risky, as you found out. Also, it'd take too much time. Why should we go to all that trouble and expense when they've got the worst of it done? The police may stir around for a few days, but they won't know anything or find out anything. Nobody will suspect anything except Crane—if he is still alive—and he won't be able to do anything."

So the argument raged. Brookings agreed with DuQuesne in aim, but would not sanction his means, holding out for quieter, more devious, less actionable methods. Finally he ended the discussion with a flat refusal and called Perkins. He told him of the larger bottle of solution; instructing him to secure it and to bring back all plans, notes, and other material pertaining to the matter in hand. Then, after giving DuQuesne an instrument like the one he himself carried, Brookings took his leave.

Late in the afternoon of the day of the explosion, Seaton came up to Crane with a mass of notes in his hand.

"I've got some of it, Mart. The power is what we figured—anything you want short of infinity. I've got the three answers you wanted most. First, the transformation is complete. No loss, no residue, no radiation or other waste. Thus, no danger and no shielding or other protection is necessary. Second, X acts only as a catalyst and is not itself consumed. Hence, an infinitesimally thin coating is all that's necessary. Third, the power is exerted as a pull along the axis of the X figure, whatever that figure is, focused at infinity.

"I also investigated those two border-line conditions. In one it generates an attractive force focused on the nearest object in line with its axis of X. In the second it's an all-out repulsion."

"Splendid, Dick." Crane thought for a minute or two. "Data enough, I think, to go ahead on. I particularly like that first border-line case. You could call it an object-compass. Focus one on the earth and we could always find our way back here, no matter how far away we get."

"Say, that's right—I never thought of anything like that. But what I came over here for was to tell you that I've got a model built that will handle me like small change. It's got more oof than a ramjet, small as it is—ten G's at least. Want to see it in action?"

"I certainly do."

As they were walking out toward the field Shiro called to them and they turned back toward the house, learning that Dorothy and her father had just arrived.

"Hello, boys." Dorothy smiled radiantly, her dimples very

much in evidence. "Dad and I came out to see how—and what—you're doing."

"You came at exactly the right time," Crane said. "Dick has built a model and was just going to demonstrate it. Come and watch."

On the field, Seaton buckled on a heavy harness, which carried numerous handles, switches, boxes, and other pieces of apparatus. He snapped the switch of the whatsitron. He then moved a slider on a flashlight-like tube which was attached to the harness by an adjustable steel cable and which he was gripping with both hands.

There was a creak of straining leather and he shot into the air for a couple of hundred feet, where he stopped and remained motionless for several seconds. Then he darted off; going forward and backward, up and down, describing zig-zags and loops and circles and figures-of-eight. After a few minutes of this display he came down in a power dive, slowing up spectacularly to a perfect landing.

"There, Oh beauteous damsel and esteemed sirs—" he began, with a low bow and a sweeping flourish, then there was a sharp snap and he was jerked sidewise off his feet. In the flourish his thumb had moved the slider a fraction of an inch and the power-tube had torn itself out of his grasp. It was now out at the full length of the cable, dragging him helplessly after it, straight toward a high stone wall.

But Seaton was helpless only for a second. Throwing his body sideways and reaching out along the taut cable, he succeeded in swinging the thing around so that he was galloping back toward the party and the field. Dorothy and her father were standing motionless, staring; Crane was running toward the shop.

"Don't touch that switch!" Seaton yelled. "I'll handle the bloody thing myself!"

At this evidence that Seaton thought himself master of the situation Crane began to laugh, but held one finger lightly on the whatsitron switch; and Dorothy, relieved of her fear, burst into a fit of the giggles. The bar was straight out in front of him, going somewhat faster than a man could normally run, swinging now right, now left as his weight was thrown from one side to the other. Seaton, dragged along like a boy holding a runaway calf by the tail, was covering the ground in prodigious leaps, at the same time pulling himself up hand over hand toward the tube. He reached it, grabbed it in both hands, again darted into the air, and came down lightly near the others, who were rocking with laughter.

"I said it would be undignified," said Seaton, somewhat short of breath, but laughing, too, "but I didn't think it would end up like this."

Dorothy seized his hand. "Are you hurt anywhere, Dick?"

"Uh-uh. Not a bit."

"I was scared green until you told Martin to lay off, but it was funny then. How about doing it again and I'll shoot it in full color?"

"Dorothy!" her father chided. "Next time it might not be funny at all."

"There'll be no next time for this rig," Seaton declared. "From here we ought to be able to go to a full-scale ship."

Dorothy and Seaton set out toward the house and Vaneman turned to Crane.

"What are you going to do with it commercially? Dick, of course, hasn't thought of anything except his spaceship. Equally of course, you have."

Crane frowned. "Yes. I've had a crew of designers working for weeks. In units of half-million to a million kilowatts we could sell power for a small fraction of a mil. However, the deeper we go into it the more likely it appears that it will make all big central power plants obsolete."

"How could that be?"

"Individual units on individual spots—but it will be some time yet before we have enough data for the machines to work on."

The evening passed rapidly. As the guests were getting ready to leave, Dorothy asked, "What are you going to call it? You both have called it forty different things this evening, and none of them were right."

"Why, 'spaceship,' of course," Seaton said.

"Oh, I didn't mean the class, I meant this particular one. There's only one possible name for her: The Skylark."

"Exactly right, Dorothy," Crane said.

"Perfect!" Seaton applauded. "And you'll christen it, Dottie, with a fifty-liter flask full of hard vacuum. 'I christen thee The Skylark—bang!'"

As an afterthought, Vaneman pulled a newspaper out of his pocket.

"Oh yes, I bought a Clarion on our way out here. It tells about an extraordinary explosion—at least, the story is extraordinary. It may not be true, but it may make interesting reading for you two scientific sharps. Good night."

Seaton walked Dorothy to the car. When he came back Crane handed him the paper without a word. Seaton read.

"It's X, all right. Not even a *Clarion* reporter could dream that up. Some poor devil tried it without my rabbit's foot in his pocket."

"But think, Dick! Something is very seriously wrong. Two people did *not* discover X at the same time. Someone stole your idea, but the idea is worthless without the metal. Where did he get it?"

"That's right. The stuff *is* extremely rare. In fact, it isn't supposed even to exist. I'd bet my case buck that we had every microgram of it known to science."

"Well, then," said the practical Crane, "We'd better find out if we have all we started with."

The storage bottle was still almost full, its seal unbroken; the vial was apparently exactly as Seaton had left it.

"It seems to be all here," Crane said.

"It can't be," Seaton declared. It's too rare—coincidence can't go that far. . . . I can tell by taking the densities."

He did so, finding that the solution in the vial was only half as strong as that in the reserve bottle.

"That's it, Mart. Somebody stole half of this vial. But he's gone where the . . . say, do you suppose . . .?"

"I do indeed. Just that."

"And the difficulty will lie in finding out which one, among the dozens of outfits who would want the stuff, is the one that actually got it?"

"Check. The idea was—must have been—taken from your demonstration. Or, rather, one man knew, from the wreckage of your laboratory, that your demonstration would not have failed had all the factors then operative been present. Who was there?"

"Oh, a lot of people came around at one time or another, but your specifications narrow the field to five men—Scott, Smith, Penfield, DuQuesne, and Roberts. Hmmm, let's see— if Scott's brain was solid cyclonite, the detonation wouldn't crack his skull; Smith is a pure theoretician; Penfield wouldn't dare quote an authority without asking permission; Du- Quesne is . . . umm . . . that is, DuQuesne isn't . . . I mean, Du—"

"DuQuesne, then, is suspect number one."

"But wait a minute! I didn't say . . ."

"Exactly. That makes him suspect number one. How about the fifth man, Roberts?"

"Not the type—definitely. He's a career man. If he got

blasted out of the Civil Service all the clocks in the city would stop."

Crane picked up his telephone and dialed.

"This is Crane. Please give me a complete report on Dr. Marc C. DuQuesne of the Rare Metals Laboratory as soon as posible. . . . Yes, full coverage . . . no limit . . . and please send two or three guards out here right now, men you can trust. . . . Thanks."

chapter **8**

SEATON AND CRANE SPENT SOME TIME IN developing the "object-compass." They made several of them, mounted in gymbals on super-shock-proof jeweled bearings. Strictly according to Seaton's Theory, the instruments were of extreme sensitivity; the one set on the smallest object at the greatest distance—a tiny glass bead at three thousand miles—registering a true line in less than one second.

Having solved the problem of navigation, they made up graduated series of "X-plosive" bullets, each one matching perfectly its standard .45-caliber counterpart. They placed their blueprints and working notes in the safe as usual, taking with them only those dealing with the object-compass and the X-plosive bullet, on which they were still working. They cautioned Shiro and the three guards to watch everything closely until they got back. Then they set out in the helicopter, to try out the new weapon in a place where the explosions could do no damage.

It came fully up to expectations. A Mark One charge, fired by Crane at a stump over a hundred yards from the flat-topped knoll that had afforded them a landing-place, tore it bodily from the ground and reduced it to splinters. The force of the explosion made the two men stagger.

"Wow!" Seaton exclaimed. "Wonder what a Mark Five will do?"

"Careful, Dick. What are you going to shoot at?"

"That rock across the valley. Range-finder says nine hundred yards. Bet me a buck I can't hit it?"

"The pistol champion of the District? Hardly!"

The pistol cracked, and when the bullet reached its destination the boulder was obliterated in a vast ball of . . . of *something*. It was not exactly—nor all—flame. It had none of the searing, killing, unbearable radiance of an atomic bomb. It did not look much, if any, hotter than the sphere of primary action of a massive charge of high explosive. It did not look, even remotely, like anything either man had ever seen before.

Their observations were interrupted by the arrival of the shock wave. They were hurled violently backward, stumbling and falling flat. When they could again keep their feet, both stared silently at the tremendous mushroom-shaped cloud which was hurling itself upward at an appalling pace and spreading itself outward almost as fast.

Crane examined Geiger and scintillometer, reporting that both had continued to register only background radiation throughout the test. Seaton made observations and used his slide rule.

"Can't do much from here, right under it, but the probable minimum is ninety-seven thousand feet and it's still boiling upward. I . . . will . . . be . . . tee . . . totally . . . jiggered."

Both men stood for minutes, awed into silence by the incredible forces they had loosed. Then Seaton made the understatement of his long life.

"I don't think I'll shoot a Mark Ten around here."

"Haven't you done anything yet?" Brookings demanded.

"I can't help it, Mr. Brookings," Perkins replied. "Prescott's men are hard to do business with."

"I know that, but surely one of them can be reached."

"Not at ten, and that was your limit. Twenty-five or no dice."

Brookings drummed fingers on desk. "Well . . . if we have to . . ." and wrote out an order on the cashier for twenty-five thousand dollars in small-to-medium bills. "I'll see you at the café, tomorrow at four o'clock."

The place referred to was the Perkins Café, a restaurant on Pennsylvania Avenue. It was the favorite eating-place of the diplomatic, political, financial, and social élite of Washington, none of whom even suspected that it had been designed and was being maintained by the world-girdling World Steel Corporation as the hub and center of its world-girdling nefarious activities.

At four o'clock of the following day Brookings was ushered into Perkins' private office.

"Blast it, Perkins, can't you do *anything?*" he demanded.

"It just couldn't be helped," Perkins replied doggedly. "Everything was figured to the second, but the Jap smelled a rat or something and jumped us. I managed to get away, but he laid Tony out cold. But don't worry—I sent Silk Humphrey and a couple of the boys out to get him. Told him to report at four oh eight. Any second now."

In less than a minute Perkins' communicator buzzed.

"This is the dick, not Silk," it said, in its tiny, tinny voice. "He's dead. So are the two goons. That Jap, he's chain lightning on greased wheels, got all three of them. Anything else I can do for you?"

"No. Your job's done." Perkins closed the switch, fusing the spy's communicator into a blob of metal; and Brookings called DuQuesne.

"Can you come to my office, or are you bugged?"

"Yes, to both. Bugged from stem to gudgeon, Prescott men in front, back, on the sides, and up in the trees. I'll be right over."

"But wait . . .!"

"Relax. D'you think they can outsmart *me?* I know more about bugging—and de-bugging—than Prescott and his dicks ever will learn."

In Brookings' office DuQuesne told, with saturnine amusement, of the devices he had rigged to misinform the private eyes. He listened to Brookings' recital of failure.

Then he said, "I knew you'd louse it up, so I've been making some plans of my own. One thing, though, I want limpidly clear. From now on I give the orders. Right?"

"Right."

"Get me a helicopter just like Crane's. Get a hophead six feet tall that weighs about a hundred and sixty pounds. Give him a three-hour jolt. Have them at the field two hours from now."

"Can do."

DuQuesne was at the field on time. So were the flying machine and the unconscious man. Both were exactly what he had ordered. He took off, climbed swiftly, made a wide circle to the west and north.

Shiro and the two guards, hearing the roar of engines, looked up and saw what they supposed to be Crane's helicopter coming down in a vertical drop. Slowing at the last possible second, it taxied up the field toward them. A man, recognizable as Seaton by his suit and physique, stood up, shouted hoarsely, pointed to the lean, still form beside him, beckoned frantically with both arms, then slumped down, completely inert.

All three rushed up to help.

There were three silenced reports and three men dropped.

DuQuesne leaped lightly out of the 'copter and scanned the three bodies. The two guards were dead, but Shiro, to his chagrin, showed faint signs of life. But very faint—he wouldn't live long.

He put on gloves, went into the house, blew the safe and rifled it. He found the vial of solution, but could find neither the larger bottle nor any reference to it. He then searched the house, from attic to basement. He found the vault, carefully concealed though its steel door was; but even he could do nothing about that. Nor was there any need, he decided, as he stood staring at it, the only change in his expression being a slight narrowing of the eyes in concentrated thought. The bulk of that solution was probably in the heaviest, deepest, safest vault in the country.

He returned to the helicopter. In a short time he was back in his own room, poring over blueprints and notebooks.

Coming in in the dusk, Crane and Seaton both began to worry when they saw that their landing lights were not burning. They made a bumpy landing and hurried toward the house. They heard a faint moan and turned, Seaton whipping out his flashlight with one hand and his automatic with the other. He hastily replaced the weapon and bent over Shiro, a touch having assured him that the other two were beyond help. They picked Shiro up and carried him into his own room. While Seaton applied first-aid treatment to the ghastly wound in Shiro's head, Crane called a surgeon, the coroner, the police, and finally Prescott, with whom he held a long conversation.

Having done all they could for the injured man, they stood by his bedside, their anger all the more deadly for being silent. Seaton stood with every muscle tense. His right hand, white-knuckled, gripped the butt of his pistol, while under his left the heavy brass rail of the bed began slowly to bend. Crane stood impassive, but with his face white and every feature hard as marble. Seaton was the first to speak.

"Mart," he gritted, husky with fury, "A man who could leave another man dying like that ain't a man at all—he's a thing. I'll shoot him with the biggest charge we've got. . . . No, I won't, either, I'll take him apart with my bare hands."

"We'll find him, Dick." Crane's voice was low, level, deadly. "That is one thing money can do."

The tension was relieved by the arrival of the surgeon and his nurses, who set to work with the deftness and precision of their highly-specialized crafts. After a time the doctor turned to Crane.

"Merely a scalp wound, Mr. Crane. He should be up in a few days."

The police, Prescott, and the coroner arrived in that order. There was a great deal of bustling, stirring about, and investigating, some of which was profitable. There were many guesses and a few sound deductions.

And Crane offered a reward of one million tax-paid dollars for information leading to the arrest and conviction of the murderer.

chapter **9**

PRESCOTT, AFTER A SLEEPLESS NIGHT, JOINED Crane and Seaton at breakfast.

"What do you make of it?" Crane asked.

"Very little, at present. Whoever did it had exactly detailed knowledge of your movements."

"Check. And you know what *that* means. The third guard, the one that escaped."

"Yes." The great detective's face grew grim. "The trouble will be proving it on him.

"Second, he was your size and build, Seaton; close enough to fool Shiro, and that would have to be ungodly close."

"DuQuesne. For all the tea in China, it was DuQuesne."

"Third, he was an expert safecracker, and that alone lets DuQuesne out. That's just as much of a specialty as yours is, and he did a beautiful job on that safe—really beautiful."

"I *still* won't buy it," Seaton insisted. "Don't forget that DuQuesne's a living encyclopedia and as much smarter than any yegg as I am than that tomcat over there. He could study safeblowing fifteen minutes and be top man in the field; and he's got guts enough to supply a regiment."

"Fourth, it *couldn't* have been DuQuesne. Everything out

there is bugged and we've had him under continuous observation. I know exactly where he has been, every minute."

"You *think* you do," Seaton corrected. "He knows more about electricity than the guy who invented it. I'm going to ask you a question. Have you ever got a man into his house?'"

"Well . . . no, not exactly . . . but that isn't necessary, these days."

"It might be, in this case. But don't try it. Unless I'm wronger than wrong, you won't."

"I'm afraid so," Prescott agreed. "But you're softening me up for something, Seaton. What is it?"

"This." Seaton placed an object-compass on the table. "I set this on him late last night, and he didn't leave his house all night—which may or may not mean a thing. That end of that needle will point at him from now on, wherever he goes and whatever comes between, and as far as I know—and I bashfully admit that I know all that's known about the thing —it can't be de-bugged. If you want to *really* know where DuQuesne is, take this and watch it. Top secret, of course."

"Of course. I'll be glad to . . . but how on earth can a thing like that work?"

After an explanation that left the common-sense-minded detective as much in the dark as before, Prescott left.

Late that evening, he joined his men at DuQuesne's house. Everything was quiet. The scientist was in his study; the speakers registered the usual faint sounds of a man absorbed in work. But after a time, and while a speaker emitted the noise of rustling papers, the needle began to move slowly— downward. Simultaneously the shadow of his unmistakable profile was thrown upon the window shade as he apparently crossed the room.

"Can't you hear him walk?" Prescott demanded.

"No. Heavy rugs—and for such a big man, he walks very lightly."

Prescott watched the needle in amazement as it dipped deeper and deeper; straight down and then behind him; as though DuQuesne had actually walked right under him! He did not quite know whether to believe it or not, nevertheless, he followed the pointing needle. It led him beside Park Road, down the hill, straight toward the long bridge which forms one entrance to Rock Creek Park. Prescott left the road and hid behind a clump of shrubbery.

The bridge trembled under the passage of a high-speed automobile, which slowed down abruptly. DuQuesne, carrying a roll of papers, scrambled up from beneath the bridge and boarded it, whereupon it resumed speed. It was of a popular make and color; and its license plates were so smeared with dirt that not even their color could be seen. The needle now pointed steadily at the distant car.

Prescott ran back to his men.

"Get your car," he told one of them. "I'll tell you where to drive as we go."

In the automobile, Prescott issued instructions by means of surreptitious glances at the compass concealed in his hand. The destination proved to be the residence of Brookings, the general manager of World Steel. Prescott told his operative to park the car somewhere and stand by; he himself settled down on watch.

After four hours a small car bearing a license number of a distant state—which was found later to be unknown to the authorities of that state—drove up; and the hidden watchers saw DuQuesne, without the papers, step into it. Knowing now what to expect, the detectives drove at high speed to the Park Road bridge and concealed themselves.

The car came up to the bridge and stopped. DuQuesne got out of it—it was too dark to recognize him by eye, but the needle pointed straight at him—and half-walked, half-slid down the embankment. He stood, a dark outline against the gray abutment. He lifted one hand above his head; a black rectangle engulfed his outline; the abutment became again a solid gray.

With his flashlight Prescott traced the almost imperceptible crack of the hidden door, and found the concealed button which DuQuesne had pressed. He did not press the button, but, deep in thought, went home to get a few hours of sleep before reporting to Crane next morning.

Both men were waiting when he appeared. Shiro, with a heavily-bandaged head, had insisted that he was perfectly able to work, and was ceremoniously ordering out of the kitchen the man who had been hired to take his place.

"Well, gentleman, your compass did the trick," and Prescott reported in full.

"I'd like to beat him to death with a club," Seaton said, savagely. "The chair's too good for him."

"Not that he is in much danger of the chair." Crane's expression was wry.

"Why, we know he did it! Surely we can prove it?"

"Knowing a thing and proving it to a jury are two entirely different breeds of cats. W haven't a shred of evidence. If we asked for an indictment we'd be laughed out of court. Check, Mr. Crane?"

"Check."

"I've bucked Steel before. They account for half my business, and for ninety-nine percent of my failures. The same thing goes for all the other agencies in town. The cops have hit them time after time with everything they've got, and simply bounced. So has the F.B.I. All any of us has been able to get is an occasional small fish."

"You think it's hopeless, then?"

"Not exactly. I'll keep on working, on my own. I owe them something for killing my men, as well as for other favors they've done me in the past. But I don't believe in holding out false hopes."

"Optimistic cuss, ain't he?" Seaton remarked as Prescott went out.

"He has cause to be, Dick. Report has it that they use murder, arson, and anything else useful in getting what they want; but they have not been caught yet."

"Well, now that we know, we're in the clear. They can't possibly get a monopoly—"

"No? You are getting the point. If we should both happen to die—accidentally, of course—then what?"

"They couldn't get away with it, Mart; you're too big. I'm small fry, but you are M. Reynolds Crane."

"No good, Dick; no good at all. Jets still crash; and so, occasionally, do egg-beaters. Worse—it does not seem to have occurred to you that World Steel is making the heavy forgings and plates for the *Skylark*."

"Hades'—brazen—bells!" Seaton was dumbfounded. "And what—if anything—can we do about *that*?"

"Very little, until after the parts get here, beyond investigating independent sources of supply."

DuQuesne and Brookings met in the Perkins Café.

"How did your independent engineers like the power-plant?"

"The report was very favorable, doctor. The stuff is all you said it was. But until we get the rest of the solution—by the way, how is the search for more X progressing?"

"Just as I told you it would—flat zero. X can't exist naturally on any planet having any significant amount of copper. Either the copper will go or the planet will, or both. Seaton's X was meteoric. It was all in one lot of platinum; and probably that one X meteor was all there ever was. However, the boys are still looking, just in case."

"Well, we'd have to get Seaton's, some day, anyway. Have you decided how to get it?"

"No. That solution is in the safest safe-deposit vault in the world, probably in Crane's name, and both keys to that box are in another one, and so on, ad infinitum. He's got to get it himself, and willingly. Not that it'd be any easier to force Seaton; but can you imagine anything strong enough to make M. Reynolds cave in now?"

"I can't say that I can . . . no. But you remarked once that your forte is direct action. How about talking with Perkins . . . no, he flopped on three tries."

"Yes, call him in. It's on execution he's weak, not planning. I'm not."

Perkins was called in, and studied the problem for many minutes. Finally he said, "There's only one way. We'll have to get a handle. . . ."

"Don't be a fool!" DuQuesne snapped. You can't get a thing on either of them—not even a frame!"

"You misunderstand, doctor. You can get a handle on any man living, if you know enough about him. Not necessarily in his past; present or future is oftentimes better. Money . . . power . . . position . . . fame. . . . women—have you considered women in this case?"

"Women, bah!" DuQuesne snorted. "Crane's been chased so long he's woman-proof, and Seaton is worse. He's engaged to Dorothy Vaneman, so he's stone blind."

"Better and better. There's your perfect handle, gentlemen; not only to the solution, but to everything else you want after Seaton and Crane have been taken out of circulation."

Brookings and DuQuesne looked at each other in perplexity. Then DuQuesne said, "All right, Perkins, after the way I popped off I'm perfectly willing to let you have a triumph. Draw us a sketch."

"Build a spaceship from Seaton's own plans and carry her off in it. Take her up out of sight—of course you'll have to have plenty of witnesses that it was a spaceship and that it did go straight up out of sight—then hide her in one of our places—say with the Spencer girl—then tell Seaton and Crane she's on Mars and will stay there till she rots if they don't come across. They'll wilt—and they wouldn't dare take a story like that to the cops. Any holes in that?"

"Not that I can see at the moment. . . ." Brookings

drummed his fingers abstractedly on the desk. "Would it make any difference if they chased us in their ship—in the condition it will be in?"

"Not a bit," DuQuesne declared. "All the better—they'll be gone, and in a wreck that will be so self-explanatory that nobody would think of making a metallurgical post-mortem."

"That's true. Who's going to drive the ship?"

"I am," DuQuesne said. "I'll need help, though. One man from the inner circle. You or Perkins. Perkins, I'd say."

"Is it safe?" Perkins asked.

"Absolutely. It's worked out to the queen's taste."

"I'll go along, then. Is that all?"

"No," Brookings replied. "You mentioned Spencer. Haven't you got that stuff away from her yet?"

"No, she's stubborn as a mule."

"Time's running out. Take her along, and don't bring her back. We'll get the stuff back some other way."

Perkins left the room; and after a long discussion of details, DuQuesne and Brookings left the restaurant, each by a different route.

chapter **10**

THE GREAT STEEL FORGINGS WHICH WERE TO form the framework of the *Skylark* arrived and were hauled into the testing room, where radium-capsule X-raying revealed flaws in every member. Seaton, after mapping the imperfections by orthometric projection, spent an hour with calipers and slide rule.

"Strong enough to stand shipment and fabrication, and maybe a little to spare—perhaps one G of acceleration while we're in the air. Any real shot of power, though, or any sudden turn, and *pop!* She collapses like a soap bubble. Want to recheck my figures?"

"No. I told you not to bother about analysis. We want sound metal, not junk."

"Ship 'em back, then—with an inspector?"

"No." At Seaton's look of surprise, Crane went on. "I've been thinking about this possibility for a long time. If we reject these forgings, they will—immediately—try to kill us some other way; and they may very well succeed. On the other hand, if we go ahead all unsuspectingly and use them, they will let us alone until the *Skylark* is done. That will give us months of free, undisturbed time. Expensive time, I grant; but worth every dollar."

"Maybe so. As the money man, you're the judge of that. But we can't fly a heap of scrap, Mart!"

"No, but while we are going ahead with this just as though we meant it, we can build another one, about four times its size, in complete secrecy."

"Mart! You're talking like a man with a paper nose! How d'you figure on keeping stuff *that* size secret from Steel?"

"It can be done. I know a chap who owns a steel mill—so insignificant, relatively speaking, that he has not been bought out or frozen out by Steel. I have helped him out from time to time, and he assures me that he will be glad to cooperate. We will not be able to oversee much of the work ourselves, which is a drawback. However, we can get MacDougall to do it for us."

"MacDougall? The man who built Intercontinental? He wouldn't touch a little job like this with a pole!"

"On the contrary, he is keen on doing it. It means building the first spaceship, you know."

"He's too big to disappear, I'd think. Wouldn't Steel follow him up?"

"They never have, a few times when he and I have been out of touch with civilization for three months at a time."

"Well, it would cost more than our whole capital."

"No more talk of money, Dick. Your contribution to the firm is worth more than everything I have."

"Hokay—if that's the way you want it, it tickles me like I'd swallowed an ostrich feather . . . and I can't think of any more objections. Four times the size—wheeeeekity-wheek! A two-hundred-pound bar—k-z-r-e-e-p-t-POWIE!

"And why don't we build an attractor—a thing like an object-compass except with a ten-pound bar instead of a needle, so if anything chases us in space we can reach out and shake the whey out of it—or machine guns shooting Mark Ones-to-Tens through pressure gaskets in the walls? I just bodaciously do NOT relish the prospect of fleeing from a gaggle of semi-intelligent alien monstrosities merely because I got nothing bigger than a rifle to fight back with."

"All you have to do is design them, Dick; and that shouldn't be too hard. But, speaking of emergencies, the power plant should really have a very large factor of safety.

Four hundred pounds, say, and everything in duplicate, from power-bars to push-buttons?"

"I'll buy that."

Work was soon begun on the huge steel shell in the independent steel plant under the direct supervision of MacDougall by men who had been in his employ for years. While it was being built, Seaton and Crane went ahead with the construction of the original spaceship. Practically all of their time, however, was spent in perfecting the many essential things that were to go into the real *Skylark*.

Thus they did not know that to the flawed members there were being attached faulty plates by imperfect welding. Nor could they have detected the poor workmanship by any ordinary inspection, for it was being done by a picked crew of experts—picked by Perkins. To make things even, Steel did not know that the many peculiar instruments installed by Seaton and Crane were not exactly what they should have been.

In due course "The Cripple"—a name which Seaton soon shortened to "Old Crip"—was finished. The foreman overheard a conversation between Crane and Seaton in which it was decided not to start for a couple of weeks, as they had to work out some kind of a book of navigation tables. Prescott reported that Steel was still sitting on its hands, waiting for the first flight. Word came from MacDougall that the *Skylark* was ready. Crane and Seaton went somewhere in the helicopter "to make a few final tests."

A few nights later a huge ball landed on Crane Field. It moved lightly, easily, betraying its thousands of tons of weight only by the hole it made in the hard-beaten ground. Seaton and Crane sprang out.

Dorothy and her father were waiting. Seaton caught her up and kissed her vigorously. Then, a look of sheerest triumph on his face, he extended a hand to Vaneman.

"She flies! *How* she flies! We've been around the moon!"

"What?" Dorothy was shocked. "Without even *telling* me? Why, I'd've been scared pea-green if I'd known!"

"That was why," Seaton assured her. "Now you won't have to worry next time we take off."

"I will so," she protested; but Seaton was listening to Vaneman.

". . . it take?"

"Not quite an hour. We could have done it in much less

"She flies like a ray of light for speed and like a bit of thistle-down for lightness. We have been around the moon!"

time." Crane's voice was calm, his face quiet; but to those
who knew him so well, every feature showed emotion.

Both inventors were at the summit, moved more than
either could have told by their achievement, by the success
of the flyer upon which they had worked so long.

Shiro broke the tension by bowing until his head almost
touched the floor. "Sirs and lady, I impel myself to state this
to be wonder extreme. If permitting I shall delightful lux-
uriate in preparation suitable refreshment."

Permission granted, he trotted away and the engineers
invited the vistors to inspect their new craft.

Although Dorothy knew what to expect, from plans and
drawings and from her own knowledge of "Old Crip," she
caught her breath as she looked about the brilliantly lighted
interior of the great sky-rover.

It was a spherical shell of hardened steel of great thickness,
some forty feet in diameter. Its true shape was not readily apparent from inside, as it was divided into levels and com-
partments by decks and walls. In its center was a spherical
structure of girders and beams. Inside this structure was a
similar one which, on smooth but immensely strong universal
bearings, was free to revolve in any direction. This inner
sphere was filled with machinery surrounding a shining copper cylinder.

Six tremendous fabricated columns radiated outward;
branching in maximum-strength design out into the hull. The
floor was heavily upholstered and was not solid; the same was
true of the dozen or more seats built in various places. There
were two instrument boards, upon which tiny lights flashed
and plate glass, plastic and metal gleamed.

Both Vanemans began to ask questions and Seaton showed
them the principal features of the novel vessel. Crane accompanied them in silence, enjoying their pleasure, glorying
in the mighty ship of space.

Seaton called attention to the great size and strength of one
of the lateral supporting columns, then led them over to the
vertical column that pierced the floor. Enormous as the
lateral was, it appeared puny beside this monster of fabricated
steel. Seaton explained that the two verticals had to be
much stronger than the four laterals, as the center of gravity
of the ship had been placed lower than its geometrical center,
so that the apparent motion of the vessel would always be
upward. Resting one hand caressingly upon the huge member,
he explained exultantly that it was the ultimately last word

in strength, made of the strongest known high-tensile, heat-treated, special-alloy steel.

"But why go to such an extreme?" the lawyer asked. "It looks as though it could support a bridge."

"It could. It'll have to, if we ever really cut loose with the power. Have you got any idea of how fast this thing can fly?"

"I have heard you talk of approaching the velocity of light, but that's a little overdrawn, isn't it?"

"Not a bit. If it wasn't for Einstein and his famous theory we could develop an acceleration twice as great as one light-velocity. As it is, we're going to see how close we can crowd it—and it'll be close, believe me. Out in space, that is. In air we'll be limited to three or four times sound, in spite of all we could do in the line of heat-exchangers and refrigeration."

"But, from what I read about jets, ten gravities for ten minutes can be fatal."

"That's right. But these floors are special, and those seats are infinitely more so. That was one of our hardest jobs; designing supporting surfaces to hold a man safe through forces that would ordinarily flatten him out into a thin layer of goo."

"I see. How are you going to steer? And how about stable reference planes to steer by? Or are you merely going to head for Mars or Venus or Neptune or Aldebaran, as the case may be?"

"That wouldn't be so good. We thought for a while we'd have to, but Mart licked it. The power plant is entirely separate from the ship, inside that inner sphere, about which the outer sphere and the ship itself are free to revolve. Even if the ship rolls or pitches, the bar stays right where it is pointed. Those six big jackets cover gyroscopes, which keep the outer sphere in exactly the same position—"

"Relative to what?" Vaneman asked. "It seems to have moved since we came in. . . . Yes, if you look closely, you can see it move."

"Naturally. Um . . . m. Never thought of it from that angle —just that its orientation isn't affected by either the ship or the power plant. If you want to pin me down, though, it's oriented solidly to the three dimensions of the steel plant at the time MacDougall got the gyroscopes up to holding speed. Since that doesn't mean much here and now, I'd say, as an approximation, that it is locked to the fixed stars. Or, rather, to the effective mass of the galaxy as a whole. . . ."

"*Please*, Dick," Dorothy interrupted. "Enough of the

jargon. Show us the important things—kitchen, bedrooms, bath."

Seaton did so, explaining in detail some of the many differences between living on earth and in a small, necessarily self-sufficient worldlet out in airless, lightless, heatless space.

"Oh, I'm just wild to go out with you, Dick. When will you take me?"

"Very soon, Dottie. Just as soon as we're sure we've got all the bugs ironed out. You'll be our first passenger, so help me."

"How do you see out? How about air and water? How do you keep warm, or cool, as the case may be?" Vaneman fired the questions as though he were cross-examining a witness. "No, excuse me; you've already mentioned the heaters and refrigerators."

"The pilots see outside, the whole sphere of vision, by means of special instruments, something like periscopes but vastly different—electronic. Passengers can see out by uncovering windows—they're made of fused quartz. We carry air—oxygen, nitrogen, helium and argon—in tanks, although we won't need much new air because of our purifiers and recovery units. We also have oxygen-generating apparatus aboard, for emergencies.

"We carry water enough to last us three months—or indefinitely if necessary, as we can recover all waste water as chemically pure H_2O. Anything else?"

"You'd better give up, dad," Dorothy advised, laughing. "It's perfectly safe for me to go along!"

"It seems to be. But it's getting pretty well along toward morning, Dorothy, and if any of us are to get any sleep at all tonight you and I should go home."

"That's so, and I'm the one who has been screaming at Dick about going to bed every night at eleven. I'll go powder my nose—I'll be right back."

Vaneman said, after Dorothy had gone, "You mentioned 'bugs' only in a very light and passing way."

"And you didn't mention them at all," Seaton countered.

"Naturally not," with a jerk of his head in the direction his daughter had taken. "How did it really go, boys?"

"Wonderful, really—" Dick began to enthuse.

"You tell me, Martin."

"In the main, very well. Of course this was a very short flight, but we found nothing wrong with the engines or their controls; we are fairly certain that no major alterations will be necessary. The optical system needs some more work; the attractors and repellors are not at all what they should be in either accuracy or delicacy. The rifles work perfectly. The air-purifiers do not remove all odors, but the air after purification is safe to breathe and physiologically adequate. The water-recovery system does not work at all—it delivers sewage."

"Well, that's not too serious, with all the water you carry."

"No, but it malfunctions so grossly that some mistake was made—obviously. It should be easy to find and to fix. For a thing so new, we both are very well satisfied with its performance."

"You're ready for Steel, then? I don't know what they'll do when they find out that you don't intend to do anything with 'Old Crip,' but they'll do something."

"I hope they blow their stacks," Seaton said, grimly. "We're ready for 'em, with a lot of stuff they never heard of and won't like a little bit. Give us four or five days to straighten out the bugs Mart told you about—then let 'em do anything they want to."

chapter 11

THE AFTERNOON FOLLOWING THE HOME-coming of the Skylark, Seaton and Dorothy returned from a long horseback ride in the park. After Seaton had mounted his motorcycle, Dorothy turned toward a bench in the shade of an old elm to watch a game of tennis on the court next door. Scarcely had she seated herself when a great copper-plated ball landed directly in front of her. A heavy steel door snapped open and a powerful figure clad in leather leaped out. The man's face and eyes were covered by his helmet flaps and amber goggles.

Dorothy leaped to her feet with a shriek—Seaton had just left her and this spaceship was far too small to be the Sky-lark—it was the counterpart of "Old Crip," which, she knew, could never fly. As these thoughts raced through her she screamed again and turned in flight; but the stranger caught her in three strides and she found herself helpless in a pair of arms as strong as Seaton's.

Picking her up lightly, DuQuesne carried her over the lawn to his spaceship. Dorothy screamed wildly as she found that her fiercest struggles made no impression on her captor. Her clawing nails glanced harmlessly off the glass and leather of his helmet; her teeth were equally ineffective against his leather coat.

With the girl in his arms DuQuesne stepped into the vessel. The door clanged shut behind them. Dorothy caught a glimpse of another woman, tied tightly into one of the side seats.

"Tie her feet, Perkins," DuQuesne ordered, holding her around the body so that her feet extended straight out in front of him. "She's a fighting wildcat."

As Perkins threw one end of a small rope around her ankles Dorothy doubled up her knees, drawing her feet as far away from him as she could. He stepped up carelessly and reached out to grasp her ankles. She straightened out viciously, driving her riding-boots into the pit of his stomach with all her strength.

It was a true solar-plexus blow; and, completely knocked out, Perkins staggered backward against the instrument-board. His outflung arm pushed the power lever out to its last notch, throwing full current through the bar, which was pointed straight up as it had been when they made their landing.

There was the creak of fabricated steel stressed almost to its limit as the vessel shot upward with a stupendous velocity, and only the ultra-protective and super-resilient properties of the floor saved their lives as they were thrown flat upon it by the awful force of their acceleration.

The maddened space-ship tore through the thin layer of the earth's atmosphere in instants—it was through it and into the almost-perfect vacuum of interplanetary space before the thick steel hull was even warmed through.

Dorothy lay flat upon her back, just as she had fallen, unable even to move her arms, gaining each breath by a terrible effort. Perkins was a huddled heap under the instrument board. The other captive, Brookings' ex-secretary, was in somewhat better case, as her bonds had snapped and she was lying in optimum position in one of the seats—forced into that position and held there, as the designer of those seats had intended. She, like Dorothy, was gasping for breath, her straining muscles barely able to force air into her lungs because of the paralyzing weight of her chest.

DuQuesne alone was able to move, and it required all of his Herculean strength to creep and crawl, snakelike, toward the instrument board. Finally, attaining his goal, he summoned all his strength to grasp, not the controlling lever, which he knew was beyond his reach, but a cutout switch only a couple of feet above his head. With a series of convulsive movements he fought his way up, first until he was crouching on elbows and knees, then into a squatting position. Then, placing his left hand under his right, he made a last supreme effort. Perspiration streamed from his face; his muscles stood out in ridges visible even under the heavy leather of his coat; his lips parted in a snarl over his locked teeth as he threw every ounce of his powerful body into an effort to force his right hand up to that switch. His hand approached it slowly—closed over it—pulled it out.

The result was startling. With the terrific power instantly cut off, and with not even the ordinary force of gravity to counteract the force DuQuesne was exerting, his own muscular effort hurled him upward, toward the center of the ship and against the instrument board. The switch, still in his grasp, was again closed. His shoulder crashed against the knobs which controlled the direction of the power bar, swinging it through a wide arc. As the ship darted off in the new direction with all its former acceleration he was hurled back against the board, tearing one end loose from its supports, and falling unconscious to the floor on the other side. After what seemed like an eternity, Dorothy and the other girl felt their senses slowly leave them.

With its four unconscious passengers the ship hurtled through empty space, its already inconceivable velocity being augmented every second by a quantity almost equal to the velocity of light—driven furiously onward by the prodigious power of the disintegrating copper bar.

Seaton had gone only a short distance from his sweetheart's home when, over the purring of his engine, he thought he heard Dorothy scream. He did not wait to make sure, but whirled his machine around and its purring changed to a bellowing roar as he opened the throttle. Gravel flew under skidding wheels as he made the turn into the Vaneman grounds at suicidal speed. He arrived at the scene just in time to see the door of the spaceship close. Before he could reach it the vessel disappeared, with nothing to mark its departure except a violent whirl of grass and sod, uprooted and carried high into the air by the vacuum of its wake. To the excited tennis players and the screaming mother of the abducted girl it seemed as though the great metal ball had vanished utterly. Only Seaton traced the line of debris in the air and saw, for a fraction of an instant, an infinitesimal black dot in the sky before it disappeared.

Interrupting the clamor of the young people, each of whom was trying to tell him what had happened, he spoke to Mrs. Vaneman rapidly but gently. "Mother, Dottie's all right. Steel's got her, but they won't keep her long. Don't worry, we'll get her. It may be a week or it may take a year; but we'll bring her back!"

He leaped upon his motorcycle and shattered all speed laws on the way to Crane's house.

"Mart!" he yelled. "They've got Dottie, in a ship made from our plans. Let's go!"

"Slow down—don't go off half-cocked. What do you plan?"

"Plan! Just chase 'em and kill 'em!"

"Which way did they go, and when?"

"Straight up. Full power. Twenty minutes ago."

"Too long ago. Straight up has moved five degrees. They may have covered a million miles, or they may have come down only a few miles away. Sit down and think—use your brain."

Seaton sat down and pulled out his pipe, fighting for self-possession. Then he jumped up and ran into his room, coming back with an object compass whose needle pointed upward.

"DuQuesne did it!" he cried, exultantly. "This is still looking right at him. Now let's go, and snap it up!"

"Not yet. How far away are they?"

Seaton touched the stud that set the needle swinging and snapped on the millisecond timer. Both men watched in strained attention as second after second went by and the needle continued to oscillate. It finally came to rest and Crane punched keys on the computer.

"Three hundred and fifty million miles. Half way out of the solar system. That means a constant acceleration of about one light."

"Nothing can go that fast, Mart. E equals M C square."

"Einstein's Theory is still a theory. This distance is an observed fact."

"And theories are modified to fit facts. Hokay. He's out of control—something went haywire."

"Undoubtedly."

"We don't know how big a bar he's got, so we can't figure how long it'll take us to catch him. For Pete's sake, Mart, let's get at it!"

They hurried out to the Skylark and made a quick check.

Seaton was closing the lock when Crane stopped him with a gesture toward the power plant.

"We have only four bars, Dick—two for each engine. It will take at least one to overtake them, and at least one to stop. If we expect to get back within our lifetime it will take the other two to get us back. Even with no allowance at all for the unexpected, we are short on power."

Seaton, though furiously eager to be off, was stopped cold. "Check. We'd better get a couple more—maybe four. We'd better load up on grub and X-plosive ammunition, too."

"And water," Crane added. "Especially water."

Seaton called the brass foundry. The manager took his order, but blandly informed him that there was not that much copper in the city, that it would be ten days or two weeks before such an order could be filled. Seaton suggested that they melt up some finished goods—bus bars and the like —price no object; but the manager was obdurate. He could not violate the priority rule.

Seaton then called other places, every place he could think of or find in the yellow pages, trying to buy anything made of copper. Bar—sheet—shapes—trolley wire—cable—house wire —anything. There was nothing available in any quantity large enough to be of any use.

After an hour of fruitless telephoning he reported, in fulminating language, to Crane.

"I'm not too surprised. Steel might not want us to have too much copper."

Sparks almost shot from Seaton's eyes. "I'm going to see Brookings. He'll give me some copper or a few of the atoms of his carcass will land in Andromeda." He started for the door.

"No, Dick, no!" Crane seized Seaton by the arm. "That wouldn't—couldn't—get us anything except indefinite delay."

"What else, then? How?"

"We can be at Wilson's in five minutes. He has some copper on hand, and can get more. The Skylark is ready to travel."

In a few minutes they were in the office of the plant in which their vessel had been built. When they had made their wants known the ironmaster shook his head.

"I'm sorry, but I don't think I've got over a hundred pounds of copper in the place, and no non-ferrous equipment. . . ."

Seaton started to explode, but Crane silenced him and told Wilson the whole story.

Wilson slammed his fist down onto his desk and roared, "I'll get copper if I have tear the roof off of the church!"

Then, more quietly, "We'll have to cobble up a furnace and crucible . . . and hand-make patterns and molds . . . and borrow a big lathe . . . but you'll get your bars just as fast as I can possibly get them out."

Two days passed before the gleaming copper cylinders were ready. During this time Crane added to their equipment every article for which he could conceive any possible use, while Seaton raged up and down in a black fury of impatience. While the bars were being loaded they made another reading on the object compass. Their faces grew tense and their hearts turned sick as minute followed minute and the needle still would not settle down. Finally, however, it came to rest. Seaton's voice almost failed him as he said, "About two hundred and thirty-five light-years. Couldn't nail the exact endpoint, but that's fairly close. They're lost like nobody was ever lost before. So long, guy." He held out his hand. "It's been mighty nice knowing you. Tell Vaneman if I come back I'll bring her with me."

Crane refused the hand. "Since when am I not going along, Dick?"

"As of just now. No sense in it. If Dottie's gone I'm going too; but M. Reynolds Crane very positively is not."

"Nonsense. This is somewhat farther than we had planned for the first trip, but there is no real difference. It is just as safe to go a thousand light-years as one, and we have ample supplies. In any event, I am going."

"Who do you think you're kidding? . . . Thanks, ace." This time, hands met in a crushing grip. "You're worth three of me."

"I'll call Vaneman," Crane said, hastily.

He did not tell the lawyer the truth, or any close approximation of it—merely that the chase would probably be longer than had been supposed, that communication could very well be impossible, that they would in all probability be gone a long time, and that he could not even guess at how long that time would be.

They closed the locks and took off. Seaton crowded on power until Crane, reading the pyrometers, warned him to cut back—the skin was getting too hot.

Free of atmosphere, Seaton again advanced the lever, notch by notch, until he could no longer support the weight of his hand, but had to resort to the arm-support designed for that emergency. He pushed the lever a few notches farther, and was forced violently down into his seat, which had automatic-

ally moved upward so that his hand still controlled the rachet
handle. Still he kept the ratchet clicking, until he knew that
he could not endure much more.

"How . . . you . . . coming?" he wheezed into his microphone. He could not really talk.

"Paas . . . s . . . sing . . . ou . . . u . . . t." Crane's reply was
barely audible. "If . . . f . . . y . . . y . . . o . . . uu
c . . . c . . . ss . . . t . . . a . . . n . . . g . . .
g . . . o . . . a . . . h . . . e . . . d . . . d . . ."

Seaton cut back a few notches. "How about this?"

"I can take this much, I think. I was right on the edge."

"I'll let her ride here, then. How long?"

"Four or five hours. Then we had better eat and take another reading."

"All right. Talking's too much work, so if it gets too much
for you, yell while you still can. I'm sure glad we're on our
way at last."

chapter **12**

FOR FORTY-EIGHT HOURS THE UNCONTROLLED
engine dragged DuQuesne's vessel through the empty reaches
of space with an awful and constantly-increasing velocity.
Then, when only a few traces of copper remained, the acceleration began to decrease. Floor and seats began to return to
their normal positions. When the last particle of copper was
gone, the ship's speed became constant. Apparently motionless to those inside her, she was in reality moving with a
velocity thousands of times greater than that of light.

DuQuesne was the first to gain control of himself. His
first effort to get up lifted him from the floor and he floated
lightly upward to the ceiling, striking it with a gentle bump
and remaining, motionless and unsupported, in the air. The
others, none of whom had attempted to move, stared at him
in amazement.

DuQuesne reached out, clutched a hand-grip, and drew
himself down to the floor. With great caution he removed his
suit, transferring two automatic pistols as he did so. By feeling gingerly of his body he found that no bones were broken.

Only then did he look around to see how his companions were faring.

They were all sitting up and holding onto something. The girls were resting quietly; Perkins was removing his leather costume.

"Good morning, Dr. DuQuesne. Something must have happened when I kicked your friend."

"Good morning, Miss Vaneman." DuQuesne smiled, more than half in relief. "Several things happened. He fell into the controls, turning on all the juice, and we left considerably faster than I intended to. I tried to get control, but couldn't. Then we all went to sleep and just woke up."

"Have you any idea where we are?"

"No . . . but I can make a fair estimate." He glanced at the empty chamber where the copper cylinder had been; took out notebook, pencil, and slide rule; and figured for minutes.

He then drew himself to one of the windows and stared out, then went to another window, and another. He seated himself at the crazily-tilted control board and studied it. He worked the computer for a few moments.

"I don't know exactly what to make of this," he told Dorothy, quietly. "Since the power was on exactly forty-eight hours, we should not be more than two light-days away from our sun. However, we certainly are. I could recognize at least some of the fixed stars and constellations from anywhere within a light-year or so of Sol, and I can't find even one familiar thing. Therefore we must have been accelerating all the time. We must be somewhere in the neighborhood of two hundred thirty-seven light-years away from home. For you two who don't know what a light-year is, about six quadrillion—six thousand million million—miles."

Dorothy's face turned white; Margaret Spencer fainted; Perkins merely goggled, his face working convulsively.

"Then we'll never get back?" Dorothy asked.

"I wouldn't say that—"

"You got us into this!" Perkins screamed, and leaped at Dorothy, murderous fury in his glare, his fingers curved into talons. Instead of reaching her, however, he merely sprawled grotesquely in the air. DuQuesne, bracing one foot against the wall and seizing a hand-grip with his left hand, knocked Perkins clear across the room with one blow of his right.

"None of that, louse," DuQuesne said, evenly. "One more wrong move out of you and I'll throw you out. It isn't her fault we're here, it's our own. And mostly yours—if you'd had three brain cells working she couldn't have kicked you. But that's past. The only thing of interest now is getting back."

"But we can't get back." Perkins whimpered. "The power's gone, the controls are wrecked, and you just said you're lost."

"I did not." DuQuesne's voice was icy. "What I said was that I don't know where we are—a different statement entirely."

"Isn't that a distinction without a difference?" Dorothy asked acidly.

"By no means, Miss Vaneman. I can repair the control board. I have two extra power bars. One of them, with direction exactly reversed, will stop us, relative to the earth. I'll burn half of the last one, then coast until, by recognizing fixed stars and triangulating them, I can fix our position. I will then know where our solar system is and will go there. In the meantime, I suggest that we have something to eat."

"A beautiful and timely thought!" Dorothy exclaimed. "I'm famished. Where's your refrigerator? But something else comes first. I'm a mess, and she must be, too. Where's our room . . . that is, we have a room?"

"Yes. That one, and there's the galley, over there. We're cramped, but you'll be able to make out. Let me say, Miss Vaneman, that I really admire your nerve. I didn't expect that lunk to disintegrate the way he did, but I thought you girls might. Miss Spencer will, yet, unless you . . ."

"I'll try to. I'm scared, of course, but falling apart won't help . . . and we've simply got to get back."

"We will. Two of us, at least."

Dorothy nudged the other girl, who had not paid any attention to anything around her, and led her along a hand-rail. As she went, she could not help but think—with more than a touch of admiration—of the man who had abducted her. Calm, cool, master of himself and the situation, disregarding completely the terrible bruises that disfigured half his face and doubtless half his body as well—she admitted to herself that it was only his example which had enabled her to maintain her self-control.

As she crawled over Perkins' suit she remembered that he had not taken any weapons from it, and a glance assured her that Perkins was not watching her. She searched it quickly, finding two automatics. She noted with relief that they were standard .45's and stuck them into her pockets.

In the room, Dorothy took one look at the other girl, then went to the galley and back.

"Here, swallow this." she ordered.

The girl did so. She shuddered uncontrollably, but did begin to come to life.

"That's better. Now, snap out of it," Dorothy said, sharply. "We aren't dead and we aren't going to be."

"I am," came the wooden reply. "You don't know that beast Perkins."

"I do so. And better yet, I know things that neither Du-Quesne nor that Perkins even guess. Two of the smartest men that ever lived are on our tail, and when they catch up with us . . . well, I wouldn't be in their shoes for anything."

"What?" Dorothy's confident words and bearing, as much the potent pill, were taking effect. The strange girl was coming back rapidly to sanity and normality. "Not really?"

"Really. We've got a lot to do, and we've got to clean up first. And with no weight . . . does it make you sick?"

"It did, dreadfully, but I've got nothing left to be sick with. Doesn't it you?"

"Not very much. I don't like it, but I'm getting used to it. And I don't suppose you know anything about it."

"No. All I can feel is that I'm falling, and it's almost unbearable."

"It isn't pleasant. I've studied it a lot—in theory—and the boys say all you've got to do is forget that falling sensation. Not that I've been able to do it, but I'm still trying. The first thing's a bath, and then—"

"A bath! Here? How?"

"Sponge-bath. I'll show you. Then . . . they brought along quite a lot of clothes to fit me, and you're just about my size . . . and you'll look nice in green. . . ."

After they had put themselves to rights, Dorothy said, "That's a lot better." Each girl looked at the other, and each liked what she saw.

The stranger was about twenty-two, with heavy, wavy black hair. Her eyes were a rich, deep brown; her skin clear, smooth ivory. Normally a beautiful girl, thought Dorothy, even though she was now thin, haggard and worn.

"Let's get acquainted before we do anything else," she said. "I'm Margaret Spencer, formerly private secretary to His High Mightiness, Brookings of Steel. They swindled my father out of an invention worth millions and then killed him. I got the job to see if I could prove it, but I didn't get much evidence before they caught me. So, after two months of things you wouldn't believe, here I am. Talking never would have done me any good, and I'm certain it won't now. Perkins will kill me . . . or maybe, if what you say is true,

I should add 'if he can.' This is the first time I've had that much hope."

"But how about Dr. DuQuesne? Surely he wouldn't let him."

"I've never met DuQuesne before, but from what I heard around the office, he's worse than Perkins—in a different way, of course. He's absolutely cold and utterly hard—a perfect fiend."

"Oh, come, you're too hard on him. Didn't you see him knock Perkins down when he came after me?"

"No—or perhaps I did, in a dim sort of way. But that doesn't mean anything. He probably wants you left alive—of course that's it, since he went to all the trouble of kidnapping you. Otherwise he would have let Perkins do anything he wanted to with you, without lifting a finger."

"I can't believe that." Nevertheless, a chill struck at Dorothy's heart as she remembered the inhuman crimes attributed to the man. "He has treated us with every consideration so far—let's hope for the best. Anyway, I'm sure we'll get back safely."

"You keep saying that. What makes you so sure?"

"Well, I'm Dorothy Vaneman, and I'm engaged to Dick Seaton, the man who invented this spaceship, and I'm as sure as can be that he is chasing us right now."

"But that's just what they want!" Margaret exclaimed. "I heard some Top Secret stuff about that. Your name and Seaton's brings it back to me. Their ship is rigged, some way or other, so it will blow up or something the first time they go anywhere!"

"That's what *they* think." Dorothy's voice dripped scorn. "Dick and his partner—you've heard of Martin Crane, of course?"

"I heard the name mentioned with Seaton's, but that's all."

"Well, he's quite a wonderful inventor, and almost as smart as Dick is. Together they found out about that sabotage and built another ship that Steel doesn't know anything about. Bigger and better and faster than this one."

"That makes me feel better." Margaret really brightened for the first time. "No matter how rough this trip will be, it'll be a vacation for me now. If I only had a gun . . ."

"Here," and as Margaret stared at the proffered weapon, "I've got another. I got them out of Perkins' suit."

"Glory be!" Margaret fairly beamed. "There *is* balm in Gilead, after all! Just watch, next time Perkins threatens to cut my heart out with his knife . . . and we'd better go make those sandwiches, don't you think? And call me Peggy, please."

"Will do, Peggy my dear—we're going to be great friends. And I'm Dot or Dottie to you."

In the galley the girls set about making dainty sandwiches, but the going was very hard indeed. Margaret was particularly inept. Slices of bread went one way, bits of butter another, ham and sausage in several others. She seized two trays and tried to trap the escaping food between them—but in the attempt she released her hold and floated helplessly into the air.

"Oh, Dot, what'll we do, anyway?" she wailed. "Everything wants to fly all over the place!"

"I don't quite know—I wish we had a bird-cage, so we could reach in and grab anything before it could escape. We'd better tie everything down, I guess, and let everybody come in and cut off a chunk of anything they want. But what I'm wondering about is drinking. I'm simply dying of thirst and I'm afraid to open this bottle." She had a bottle of ginger ale clutched in her left hand, an opener in her right; one leg was hooked around a vertical rail. "I'm afraid it'll go into a million drops and Dick says if you breathe them in you're apt to choke to death."

"Seaton was right—as usual." Dorothy whirled around. DuQuesne was surveying the room, a glint of amusement in his one sound eye. "I wouldn't recommend playing with charged drinks while weightless. Just a minute—I'll get the net."

He got it; and while he was deftly clearing the air of floating items of food he went on. "Charged stuff could be murderous unless you're wearing a mask. Plain liquids you can drink through a straw, after you learn how. Your swallowing has got to be conscious and all muscular with no gravity. But what I came here for was to tell you I'm ready to put on one G of acceleration so we'll have normal gravity. I'll put it on easy, but watch it."

"What a *heavenly* relief!" Margaret cried, when everything again stayed put. "I never thought I'd ever be grateful for just being able to stand still in one place, did you?"

Preparing the meal was now of course simple enough. As the four ate, Dorothy noticed that DuQuesne's left arm was almost useless and that he ate with difficulty because of his terribly bruised face. After the meal was done she went to the medicine chest and selected containers, swabs, and gauze.

"Come over here, doctor. First aid is indicated."

"I'm all right . . ." he began, but at her imperious gesture he got up carefully and came toward her.

"Your arm is lame. Where's the damage?"

"The shoulder is the worst. I rammed it through the board."

"Take off your shirt and lie down here."

He did so and Dorothy gasped at the extent and severity of the man's injuries.

"Will you get me some towels and hot water, please, Peggy?" She worked busily for minutes, bathing away clotted blood, applying antiseptics, and bandaging. "Now for those bruises—I never saw anything like them before. I'm not really a nurse. What would you use? Tripidiagen or . . ."

"Amylophene. Massage it in as I move the arm."

He did not wince and his expression did not change; but he began to sweat and his face turned white. She paused.

"Keep it up, nurse," he directed, coolly. "That stuff's murder in the first degree, but it does the job and it's fast."

When she had finished and he was putting his shirt back on: "Thanks, Miss Vaneman—thanks a lot. It feels a hundred per cent better already. But why did you do it? I'd think you'd want to bash me with that basin instead."

"Efficiency." She smiled. "As our chief engineer it won't do to have you laid up."

"Logical enough, in a way . . . but . . . I wonder . . ."

She did not reply, but turned to Perkins.

"How are you, Mr. Perkins? Do you require medical attention?"

"No," Perkins growled. "Keep away from me or I'll cut your heart out."

"Shut up!" DuQuesne snapped.

"I haven't done anything!"

"Maybe it didn't quite constitute making a break, so I'll broaden the definition. If you can't talk like a man, keep still. Lay off Miss Vaneman—thoughts, words, and actions. I'm in charge of her and I will have no interference whatever. This is your last warning."

"How about Spencer, then?"

"She's your responsibility, not mine."

An evil light appeared in Perkins' eyes. He took out a wicked-looking knife and began to strop it carefully on the leather of the seat, glaring at his victim the while.

Dorothy started to protest, but was silenced by a gesture from Margaret, who calmly took the pistol out of her pocket. She jerked the slide and held the weapon up on one finger.

"Don't worry about his knife. He's been sharpening it for

my benefit for the last month. It doesn't mean a thing. But you shouldn't play with it so much, Perkins, you might be tempted to try to throw it. So drop it in the floor and kick it over here to me. Before I count three. One." The heavy pistol steadied into line with his chest and her finger tightened on the trigger.

"Two." Perkins obeyed and Margaret picked up the knife.

"Doctor!" Perkins appealed to DuQuesne, who had watched the scene unmoved, a faint smile upon his saturnine face. "Why don't you shoot her? You won't sit there and see me murdered!"

"Won't I? It makes no difference to me which of you kills the other, or if you both do, or neither. You brought this on yourself. Anyone with any fraction of a brain doesn't leave guns lying around loose. You should have seen Miss Vaneman take them—I did."

"You saw her take them and didn't warn me?" Perkins croaked.

"Certainly. If you can't take care of yourself I'm not going to take care of you. Especially after the way you bungled the job. I could have recovered the stuff she stole from that ass Brookings inside an hour."

"How?" Perkins sneered. "If you're so good, why did you have to come to me about Seaton and Crane?"

"Because my methods wouldn't work and yours would. It isn't on planning that you're weak, as I told Brookings—it's on execution."

"Well, what are you going to do about her? Are you going to sit there and lecture all day?"

"I am going to do nothing whatever. Fight your own battles."

Dorothy broke the silence that followed. "You did see me take the guns, doctor?"

"I did. You have one in your right breeches pocket now."

"Then why didn't you, or don't you, try to take it away from me?" she asked, wonderingly.

" 'Try' is the wrong word. If I had not wanted you to take them you wouldn't have. If I didn't want you to have a gun now I would take it away from you," and his black eyes stared into her violet ones with such calm certainty that she felt her heart sink.

"Has Perkins got any more knives or guns or things in his room?" Dorothy demanded.

"I don't know," indifferently. Then, as both girls started for Perkins' room DuQuesne rapped out, "Sit down, Miss

Vaneman. Let them fight it out. Perkins has his orders about you; I'm giving you orders about him. If he oversteps, shoot him. Otherwise, hands off completely—in every respect."

Dorothy threw up her head in defiance; but, meeting his cold stare, she paused irresolutely and sat down, while the other girl went on.

"That's better," DuQuesne said. "Besides, it would be my guess that she doesn't need any help."

Margaret returned from the search and thrust her pistol back into her pocket. "That ends that," she declared. "Are you going to behave yourself or do I chain you by the neck to a post?"

"I suppose I'll have to, if the doc's gone back on me," Perkins snarled. "But I'll get you when we get back, you—"

"Stop it!" Margaret snapped. "Now listen. Call me names any more and I'll start shooting. One name, one shot; two names, two shots; and so on. Each shot in a carefully selected place. Go ahead."

DuQuesne broke the silence that followed. "Well, now that the battle's over and we're fed and rested, I'll put on some power. Everybody into seats."

For sixty hours he drove through space, reducing the acceleration only at mealtimes, when they ate and exercised their stiffened, tormented bodies. The power was not cut down for sleep; everyone slept as best he could.

Dorothy and Margaret were together constantly and a real intimacy grew up between them. Perkins was for the most part sullenly quiet. DuQuesne worked steadily during all his waking hours, except at mealtimes when he talked easily and well. There was no animosity in his bearing or in his words; but his discipline was strict and his reproofs merciless.

When the power bar was exhausted DuQuesne lifted the sole remaining cylinder into the engine, remarking:

"Well, we should be approximately stationary, relative to Earth. Now we'll start back."

He advanced the lever, and for many hours the regular routine of the ship went on. Then DuQuesne, on waking, saw that the engine was no longer perpendicular to the floor, but was inclined slightly. He read the angle of inclination on the great circles, then scanned a sector of space. He reduced the current, whereupon all four felt a lurch as the angle was increased many degrees. He read the new angle hastily and restored touring power. He then sat down at the computer and figured—with that much power on, a tremendous and unnerving job.

"What's the matter, doctor?" Dorothy asked.

"We're being deflected a little from our course."

"Is that bad?"

"Ordinarily, no. Every time we pass a star its gravity pulls us a little out of line. But the effects are slight, do not last long, and tend to cancel each other out. This is too big and has lasted altogether too long. If it keeps on, we could miss the solar system altogether; and I can't find anything to account for it."

He watched the bar anxiously, expecting to see it swing back into the vertical, but the angle grew steadily larger. He again reduced the current and searched the heavens for the troublesome body.

"Do you see it yet?" Dorothy asked, apprehensively.

"No . . . but this optical system could be improved. I could do better with night-glasses, I think."

He brought out a pair of grotesque-looking binoculars and stared through them out of an upper window for perhaps five minutes.

"Good God!" he exclaimed. "It's a dead star and we're almost onto it!"

Springing to the board, he whirled the bar into and through the vertical, then measured the apparent diameter of the strange object. Then, after cautioning the others, he put on more power than he had been using. After exactly fifteen minutes he slackened off and made another reading. Seeing his expression, Dorothy was about to speak, but he forestalled her.

"We lost more ground. It must be a lot bigger than anything known to our astronomers. And I'm not trying to pull away from it; just to make an orbit around it. We'll have to put on full power—take seats!"

He left full power on until the bar was nearly gone and made another series of observations. "Not enough," he said, quietly.

Perkins screamed and flung himself upon the floor; Margaret clutched at her heart with both hands; Dorothy, though her eyes looked like black holes in her white face, looked at him steadily and asked, "This is the end, then?"

"Not yet." His voice was calm and level. "It'll take two days, more or less, to fall that far, and we have a little copper left for one last shot. I'm going to figure the angle to make that last shot as effective as possible."

"Won't the repulsive outer coating do any good?"

"No; it'll be gone long before we hit. I'd strip it and feed it to the engine if I could think of a way of getting it off."

He lit a cigarette and sat at ease at the computer. He sat there, smoking and computing, for over an hour. He then changed, very slightly, the angle of the engine.

"Now we look for copper," he said. "There isn't any in the ship itself—everything electrical is silver, down to our flashlights and the bases of the lamps. But examine the furnishings and all your personal stuff—*anything* with copper or brass in it. That includes metallic money—pennies, nickles, and silver."

They found a few items, but very few. DuQuesne added his watch, his heavy signet ring, his keys, his tie-clasp, and the cartridges from his pistol. He made sure that Perkins did not hold anything out. The girls gave up not only their money and cartridges but their jewelry, including Dorothy's engagement ring.

"I'd like to keep it, but . . ." She said, as she added it to the collection.

"Everything goes that has any copper in it; and I'm glad Seaton's too much of a scientist to buy platinum jewelry. But, if we get away, I doubt very much if you'll be able to see any difference in your ring. Very little copper in it—but we need every milligram we can get."

He threw all the metal into the power chamber and advanced the lever. It was soon spent; and after the final observation, while the others waited in suspense, he made his curt announcement.

"Not quite enough."

Perkins, his mind already weakened, went completely insane. With a wild howl he threw himself at the unmoved scientist, who struck him on the head with the butt of his pistol as he leaped. The force of the blow crushed Perkin's head and drove his body to the other side of the ship. Margaret looked as though she were about to faint. Dorothy and DuQuesne looked at each other. To the girl's amazement the man was as calm as though he were in his own room at home on earth. She made an effort to hold her voice steady. "What next, doctor?"

"I don't exactly know. I still haven't been able to work out a method of recovering that plating . . . It's so thin that there isn't much copper, even on a sphere as big as this one."

"Even if you could get it, and it were enough, we'd starve

anyway, wouldn't we?" Margaret, holding herself together desperately, tried to speak lightly.

"Not necessarily. That would give me time to figure out something else to do."

"You wouldn't have to figure anything else," Dorothy declared. "Maybe you won't, anyway. You said we have two days?"

"My observations were crude, but it's a little over two days—about forty-nine and a half hours now. Why?"

"Because Dick and Martin Crane will find us before very long. Quite possibly within two days."

"Not in this life. If they tried to follow us they're both dead now."

"That's where even you are wrong!" she flashed. "They knew all the time exactly what you were doing to our old Skylark, so they built another one, that you never knew anything about. And they know a lot about this new metal that you never heard of, too, because it wasn't in those plans you stole!"

DuQuesne went directly to the heart of the matter, paying no attention to her barbs. "Can they follow us in space without seeing us?" he demanded.

"Yes. At least, I think they can."

"How do they do it?"

"I don't know. I wouldn't tell you, if I did!"

"You think not? I won't argue the point at the moment. If they can find us—which I doubt—I hope they detect this dead star in time to keep away from it—and us."

"But why?" Dorothy gasped. "You've been trying to kill both of them—wouldn't you be glad to take them with us?"

"Please try to be logical. Far from it. There's no connection. I tried to kill them, yes, because they stood in the way of my development of this new metal. If, however, I am not going to be the one to do it—I certainly hope Seaton goes ahead with it. It's the greatest discovery ever made, bar none; and if both Seaton and I, the only two men able to develop it properly, get killed it will be lost, perhaps for hundreds of years."

"If he must go, too, I hope he doesn't find us . . . but I don't believe it. I simply know he could get us away from here."

She continued more slowly, almost speaking to herself, her heart sinking with her voice, "He's following us and he won't stop even if he knows he can't get away."

"There's no denying the fact that our situation is critical;

but as long as I'm alive I can think. I'm going to dope out
some way of getting that copper."

"I hope you do." Dorothy kept her voice from breaking
only by a tremendous effort. "I see Peggy's fainted. I wish
I could. I'm worn out."

She drew herself down upon one of the seats and stared
at the ceiling, fighting an almost overpowering impulse to
scream.

Thus time wore on—Perkins dead; Margaret unconscious;
Dorothy lying in her seat, her thoughts a formless prayer,
buoyed only by her faith in God and in her lover; DuQuesne
self-possessed, smoking innumerable cigarettes, his keen mind
at grips with its most desperate problem, grimly fighting until
the very last instant of life—while the powerless spaceship
fell with an appalling velocity, and faster and yet faster,
toward that cold and desolate monster of the heavens.

chapter **13**

SEATON AND CRANE DROVE THE SKYLARK AT
high acceleration in the direction indicated by the unwavering
compass, each man taking a twelve-hour trick at the board.

The *Skylark* justified the faith of her builders, and the two
inventors, with an exultant certainty of success, flew out
beyond man's wildest imaginings. Had it not been for the
haunting fear for Dorothy's safety, the journey would have
been one of pure triumph, and even that anxiety did not
preclude a profound joy in the enterprise.

"If that misguided ape thinks he can pull a stunt like
that and get away with it he's got another think coming,"
Seaton declared, after making a reading on the other ship
after a few days of flight. "He went off half-cocked for sure
this time, and we've got him right where the hair is short.
Only about a hundred light-years now. Better we reverse
pretty quick, you think?"

"It's hard to say—very hard. By our dead reckoning he
seems to have started back; but dead reckoning is notoriously
poor reckoning and we have no reference points."

"Well, dead reckoning's the only thing we've got, and

anyway you can't be a precisionist out here. A light-year plus or minus won't make any difference."

"No, I suppose not," and Crane read off the settings which, had his data been exact, would put the *Skylark* in exactly the same spot with, and having exactly the same velocity as, the other space-ship at the point of meeting.

The big ship spun, with a sickening lurch, through a half-circle as the bar was reversed. They knew that they were traveling in a direction that seemed "down," even though they still seemed to be going "up."

"Mart! C'mere."

"Here."

"We're getting a deflection. Too big for a star—unless it's another S-Doradus—and I can't see a thing—theoretically, of course, it could be anywhere to starboard. I want a check, fast, on true course and velocity. Is there any way to measure a gravity field you're falling freely in without knowing any distances? Any kind of an approximation would help."

Crane observed, computed, and reported that the *Skylark* was being very strongly attracted by some object almost straight ahead.

"We'd better break out the big night-glasses and take a good look—as you said, this optical system could have more power. But how far away are they?"

"A few minutes over ten hours."

"Ouch! Not good . . . veree ungood, in fact. By pouring it on, we could make it three or four hours . . . but . . . even so . . . you . . ."

"Even so. Me. We're in this together, Dick; all the way. Just pour it on."

As the time of meeting drew near they took readings every minute. Seaton juggled the power until they were very close to the other vessel and riding with it, then killed his engine. Both men hurried to the bottom port with their night-glasses and stared into star-studded blackness.

"Of course," Seaton argued as he stared, "it is theoretically possible that a body can exist large enough to exert this much force and not show a disk, but I don't believe it. Give me four or five minutes of visual angle and I'll buy it, but—"

"There!" Crane broke in. "At least half a degree of visual angle. Eleven o'clock, fairly high. Not bright, but dark. Almost invisible."

"Got it. And that little black spot, just inside the edge at half past four—DuQuesne's job?"

"I think so. Nothing else in sight."

"Let's grab it and get out of here while we're all in one piece!"

In seconds they reduced the distance until they could plainly see the other vessel: a small black circle against the somewhat lighter black of the dead star. Crane turned on the searchlight. Seaton focused their heaviest attractor and gave it everything it would take. Crane loaded a belt of solid ammunition and began to fire peculiarly-spaced bursts.

After an interminable silence DuQuesne drew himself out of his seat. He took a long drag at his cigarette, deposited the butt carefully in an ashtray, and put on his space-suit; leaving the faceplates open.

"I'm going after that copper, Miss Vaneman. I don't know exactly how much of it I'll be able to recover, but I hope . . ."

Light flooded in through a port. DuQuesne was thrown flat as the ship was jerked out of free fall. They heard an insistent metallic tapping, which DuQuesne recognized instantly.

"A machine gun!" he blurted in amazement. "What in . . . wait a minute, that's Morse! A–R–E—are . . . Y–O–U— you . . . A—L—I—V—E—alive. . . ."

"It's Dick!" Dorothy screamed. "He's found us—I knew he would! You couldn't beat Dick and Martin in a thousand years!"

The two girls locked their arms around each other in a hysterical outburst of relief; Margaret's incoherent words and Dorothy's praises of her lover mingled with their racking sobs.

DuQuesne had climbed to the upper port; had unshielded it. "S–O–S" he signalled with his flashlight.

The searchlight died. W–E K–N–O–W. P–A–R–T–Y O–K–?" It was a light this time, not bullets.

"O–K" DuQuesne knew what "Party" meant—Perkins did not count.

"S–U–I–T–S–?"

"Y—E–S"

"W—I—L—L T—O—U—C—H L—O—C—K T—O L—O—C—K B—R—A—C—E S—E—L—V—E—S."

"O–K"

DuQuesne reported briefly to the two girls. All three put on space-suits and crowded into the tiny airlock. The lock was pumped down. There was a terrific jar as the two ships of space were brought together and held together. Outer valves opened; residual air screamed out into the interstellar void. Moisture condensed upon glass, rendering sight useless.

"Blast!" Seaton's voice came tinnily over the helmet radios. "I can't see a foot. Can you, DuQuesne?"

"No, and these joints don't move more than a couple of inches."

"These suits need a lot more work. We'll have to go by feel. Pass 'em along."

DuQuesne grabbed the girl nearest him and shoved her toward the spot where Seaton would have to be. Seaton seized her, straightened her up, and did his heroic best to compress that suit until he could at least feel his sweetheart's form.

He was very much astonished to feel motions of resistance and to hear a strange voice cry out, "Don't! It's me! Dottie's next!"

She was, and she put as much fervor into the reunion as he did. As a lovers' embrace it was unsatisfactory; but it was an eager, if distant, contact.

DuQuesne dived through the opening; Crane groped for the controls that closed the lock. Pressure and temperature came back up to normal. The clumsy suits were taken off. Seaton and Dorothy went into each other's arms.

And this time it was a real lovers' embrace.

"We'd better start doing something," came DuQuesne's incisive voice. "Every minute counts."

"One thing first," Crane said. "Dick, what shall we do with this murderer?"

Seaton, who had temporarily forgotten all about DuQuesne, whirled around.

"Chuck him back into his own tub and let him go to the devil!" he said, savagely.

"Oh, no, Dick!" Dorothy protested, seizing his arm. "He treated us very well, and saved my life once. Besides, you can't become a cold-blooded murderer just because he is. You know you can't."

"Maybe not . . . Okay, I won't kill him—unless he gives me about half an excuse . . . maybe."

"Out of the question, Dick," Crane decided. "Perhaps he can earn his way?"

"Could be." Seaton thought for a moment, his face still grim and hard. "He's smart as Satan and strong as a bull . . . and if there's any possible one thing he is not, it's a liar."

He faced DuQuesne squarely, gray eyes boring into eyes

of midnight black. "Will you give us your word to act as one of the party?"

"Yes." DuQuesne stared back unflinchingly. His expression of cold unconcern had not changed throughout the conversation: it did not change now. "With the understanding that I reserve the right to leave you at any time— 'escape' is a melodramatic word, but fits the facts closely enough—provided I can do so without affecting unfavorably your ship, your project then in work, or your persons collectively or individually."

"You're the lawyer, Mart. Does that cover it?"

"Admirably." Crane said. "Fully yet concisely. Also, the fact of the reservation indicates that he means it."

"You're in, then," Seaton said to DuQuesne, but he did not offer to shake hands. "You've got the dope. What'll we have to put on to get away?"

"You can't pull straight away—and live—but . . ."

"Sure we can. Our power-plant can be doubled in emergencies."

"I said 'and live.'" Seaton, remembering what one full power was like, kept still.

"The best you can do is a hyperbolic orbit, and my guess is that it'll take full power to make that. Ten pounds more copper might have given me a graze, but we're a lot closer now. You've got more and larger tools than I had, Crane. Do you want to recompute it now, or give it a good, heavy shot and then figure it?"

"A shot, I think. What do you suggest?"

"Set your engine to roll for a hyperbolic and give it full drive for . . . say an hour."

"Full power." Crane said, thoughtfully. "I can't take that much. But if—"

"I can't, either," Dorothy said, foreboding in her eyes. "Nor Margaret."

"—full power is necessary," Crane continued as though the girl had not spoken, "full power it shall be. Is it really of the essence, DuQuesne?"

"Definitely. More than full would be better. And it's getting worse every minute."

"How much power can you take?" Seaton asked.

"More than full. Not much more, but a little."

"If you can, I can." Seaton was not boasting, merely stating a fact. "So here's what let's do. Double the engines up. DuQuesne and I will notch the power up until one of us has to quit. Run an hour on that, and then read the news. Check?"

"Check," said Crane and DuQuesne simultaneously, and the three men set furiously to work. Crane went to the engines, DuQuesne to the observatory. Seaton rigged helmets to air- and oxygen-tanks through valves on his board.

Seaton placed Margaret upon a seat, fitted a helmet over her head, strapped her in, and turned to Dorothy.

Instantly they were in each other's arms. He felt her labored breathing and the hard beating of her heart; saw the fear of the unknown in the violet depths of her eyes; but she looked at him steadily as she said: "Dick, sweetheart, if this is good-bye . . ."

"It isn't, Dottie—yet—but I know . . ."

Crane and DuQuesne had finished their tasks, so Seaton hastily finished his job on Dorothy. Crane put himself to bed; Seaton and DuQuesne put on their helmets and took their places at the twin boards.

In quick succession twenty notches of power went on. The *Skylark* leaped away from the other ship, which continued its mad fall—a helpless hulk, manned by a corpse, falling to destruction upon the bleak surface of a dead star.

Notch by notch, slower now, the power went up. Seaton turned the mixing valve, a little with each notch, until the oxygen concentration was as high as they had dared to risk.

As each of the two men was determined that he would make the last advance, the duel continued longer than either would have believed possible. Seaton made what he was sure was his final effort and waited—only to feel, after a minute, the surge of the vessel that told him that DuQuesne was still able to move.

He could not move any part of his body, which was oppressed by a sickening weight. His utmost efforts to breathe forced only a little oxygen into his lungs. He wondered how long he could retain consciousness under such stress. Nevertheless, he put out everything he had and got one more notch. Then he stared at the clock-face above his head, knowing that he was all done and wondering whether DuQuesne could put on one more notch.

Minute after minute went by and the acceleration remained constant. Seaton, knowing that he was now in sole charge of the situation, fought off unconsciousness while the sweep-hand of the clock went around and around.

After an eternity of time sixty minutes had passed and Seaton tried to cut down his power, only to find that the long strain had so weakened him that he could not reverse the ratchet. He was barely able to give the lever the backward jerk which broke contact completely. Safety straps creaked as, half the power shut off, the suddenly released springs tried to hurl five bodies upward.

DuQuesne revived and shut down his engine. "You're a better man than I am, Gunga Din," he said, as he began to make observations.

"Because you were so badly bunged up, is all—one more notch would've pulled my cork," and Seaton went over to liberate Dorothy and the stranger.

Crane and DuQuesne finished their computations.

"Did we gain enough?" Seaton asked.

"More than enough. One engine will take us past it."

Then, as Crane still frowned in thought, DuQuesne went on:

"Don't you check me, Crane?"

"Yes and no. Past it, yes, but not safely past. One thing neither of us thought of, apparently—Roche's Limit."

"That wouldn't apply to this ship," Seaton said, positively. "High-tensile alloy steel wouldn't crumble."

"It might," DuQuesne said. "Close enough, it would. . . . What mass would you assume, Crane—the theoretical maximum?"

"I would. That star may not be that, quite, but it isn't far from it." Both men again bent over their computers.

"I make it thirty-nine point seven notches of power, doubled," DuQuesne said, when he had finished. "Check?"

"Closely enough—point six five," Crane replied.

"Forty notches . . . Ummm . . ." DuQuesne paused. "I went out at thirty-two. . . . That means an automatic advance. It'll take time, but it's the only. . . ."

"We've got it already—all we have to do is set it. But that'll take an ungodly lot of copper and what'll we do to live through it? Plus pressure on the oxygen? Or what?"

After a short but intense consultation the men took all the steps they could to enable the whole party to live through what was coming. Whether they could do enough no one knew. Where they might lie at the end of this wild dash for safety; how they were to retrace their way with their depleted supply of copper, what other dangers of dead star, sun, or planet lay in their path, were terrifying questions that had to be ignored.

DuQuesne was the only member of the party who actually

felt any calmness, the quiet of the others expressing their courage in facing fear.

The men took their places. Seaton started the motor which would automatically advance both power levers exactly forty notches and then stop.

Margaret Spencer was the first to lose consciousness. Soon afterward, Dorothy stifled an impulse to scream as she felt herself going under. A half-minute later and Crane went out, calmly analyzing his sensations to the last. Shortly thereafter DuQuesne also lapsed into unconsciousness, making no effort to avoid it, as he knew that it would make no difference in the end.

Seaton, though he knew it was useless, fought to keep his senses as long as possible, counting the impulses as the levers were advanced.

Thirty-two. He felt the same as when he had advanced his lever for the last time.

Thirty-three. A giant hand shut off his breath, although he was fighting to the utmost for air. An intolerable weight rested upon his eyeballs, forcing them back into his head. The universe whirled about him in dizzy circles; orange and black and green stars flashed before his bursting eyes.

Thirty-four. The stars became more brilliant and of more wildly variegated colors, and a giant pen dipped in fire wrote equations and symbols upon his quivering brain.

Thirty-five. The stars and the fiery pen exploded in pyrotechnic coruscation of searing, blinding light and he plunged into a black abyss.

Faster and faster the Skylark hurtled downward in her not-quite-hyperbolic path. Faster and faster, as minute by minute went by, she came closer and closer to that huge dead star. Eighteen hours from the start of that fantastic drop she swung around it in the tightest, hardest conceivable arc. Beyond Roche's Limit, it is true, but so very little beyond it that Martin Crane's hair would have stood on end if he had known.

Then, on the back leg of that incomprehensibly gigantic swing, the forty notches of doubled power began really to take hold. At thirty-six hours her path was no longer even approximately hyperbolic. Instead of slowing down, relative to the dead star that held her in an ever-weaking grip, she was speeding up at a tremendous rate.

At two days, that grip was very weak.

At three days the monster she had left was having no measurable effect.

Hurtled upward, onward, outward by the inconceivable power of the unleashed copper demons in her center, the *Skylark* tore through the reaches of interstellar space with an unthinkable, almost incalculable velocity, beside which the velocity of light was as that of a snail to that of a rifle bullet.

chapter 14

SEATON OPENED HIS EYES AND GAZED ABOUT about him wonderingly. Only half conscious, bruised and sore in every part, he could not remember what had happened. Instinctively drawing a deep breath, he coughed as the plus-pressure gas filled his lungs, bringing with it a complete understanding of the situation. He tore off his helmet and drew himself across to Dorothy's couch.

She was still alive!

He placed her face downward upon the floor and began artificial respiration. Soon he was rewarded by the coughing he had longed to hear. Snatching off her helmet, he seized her in his arms, while she sobbed convulsively on his shoulder. The first ecstacy of their greeting over, she started guiltily.

"Oh, Dick! See about Peggy—I wonder if . . ."

"Never mind," Crane said. "She is doing nicely."

Crane had already revived the stranger. DuQuesne was nowhere in sight. Dorothy blushed vividly and disengaged her arms from around Seaton's neck. Seaton, also blushing, dropped his arms and Dorothy floated away, clutching frantically at a hand-hold just out of her reach.

"Pull me down, Dick!" Dorothy laughed.

Seaton grabbed her ankle unthinkingly, neglecting his own anchorage, and they floated in the air together. Martin and Margaret, each holding a line, laughed heartily.

"Tweet, tweet—I'm a canary," Seaton said, flapping his arms. "Toss us a line, Mart."

"A Dicky-bird, you mean," Dorothy said.

Crane studied the floating pair with mock gravity.

"That is a peculiar pose, Dick. What is it supposed to represent—Zeus sitting on his throne?"

"I'll sit on your neck, you lug, if you don't get a wiggle on with that rope!"

As he spoke, however he came within reach of the ceiling, and could push himself and his companion to a line.

Seaton put a bar into one of the engines and, after flashing the warning light, applied a little power. The *Skylark* seemed to leap under them; then everything had its normal weight once more.

"Now that things have settled down a little," Dorothy said, "I'll introduce you two to Miss Margaret Spencer, a very good friend of mine. These are the boys I told you so much about, Peggy. This is Dr. Dick Seaton, my fiancé. He knows everything there is to be known about atoms, electrons, neutrons, and so forth. And this is Mr. Martin Crane, who is a simply wonderful inventor. He made all these engines and things."

"I may have heard of Mr. Crane," Margaret said, eagerly. "My father was an inventor, too, and he used to talk about a man named Crane who invented a lot of instruments for supersonic planes. He said they revolutionized flying. I wonder if you are that Mr. Crane?"

"That is unjustifiedly high praise, Miss Spencer," Crane replied, uncomfortable, "but as I have done a few things along that line I could be the man he referred to."

"If I may change the subject," Seaton said, "where's Du-Quesne?"

"He went to clean up. Then he was going to the galley to check damage and see about something to eat."

"Stout fella!" Dorothy applauded. "Food! And *especially* about cleaning up—if you know what I mean and I think you do. Come on, Peggy, I know where our room is."

"What a girl!" Seaton said as the women left, Dorothy half-supporting her companion. "She's bruised and beat up from one end to the other. She's more than half dead yet—she didn't have enough life left in her to flag a hand-car. She can't even walk; she can just barely hobble. And did she let out one single yip? I ask to know. 'Business as usual,' all the way, if it kills her. What a girl!"

"Include Miss Spencer in that, too, Dick. Did she 'let out any yips'? And she was not in nearly as good shape as Dorothy was, to start with."

"That's right," Seaton agreed, wonderingly. "She's got plenty of guts, too. Those two women, Marty my old and stinky chum, are blinding flashes and deafening reports. . . .

Well, let's go get a bath and shave. And shove the air-conditioners up a couple of notches, will you?"

When they came back they found the two girls seated at one of the ports. "Did you dope yourself up, Dot?" Seaton asked.

"Yes, both of us. With amylophene. I'm getting to be a slave to the stuff." She made a wry face.

Seaton grimaced too. "So did we. Ouch! Nice stuff that amylophene."

"But come over here and look out of this window. Did you ever see anything like it?"

As the four heads bent, so close together, an awed silence fell upon the little group. For the blackness of the black of the interstellar void is not the darkness of an earthly night, but the absolute absence of light—a black beside which that of platinum dust is merely gray. Upon this indescribably black backdrop there glowed faint patches which were nebulae; there blazed hard, brilliant, multi-colored, dimensionless points of light which were stars.

"Jewels on black velvet," Dorothy breathed. "Oh, gorgeous . . . wonderful!"

Through their wonder a thought struck Seaton. He leaped to the board. "Look here, Mart. I didn't recognize a thing out there and I wondered why. We're heading away from the earth and we must be making plenty of light-speeds. The swing around that big dud was really something, of course, but the engine should have . . . or should it?"

"I think not. . . . Unexpected, but not a surprise. That close to Roche's Limit, anything might happen."

"And did, I guess. We'll have to check for permanent deformations. But this object-compass still works—let's see how far we are away from home."

They took a reading and both men figured the distance.

"What d'you make it, Mart? I'm afraid to tell you my result."

"Forty-six point twenty-seven light-centuries. Check?"

"Check. We're up the well-known creek without a paddle. . . . The time was twenty-three thirty-two by the chronometer—good thing you built it to stand going through a stone-crusher. My watch's a total loss. They all are, I imagine. We'll read it again in an hour or so and see how fast we're going. I'll be scared witless to say that figure out loud, too."

"Dinner is announced," said DuQuesne, who had been standing at the door, listening.

The wanderers, battered, stiff and sore, seated themselves

at a folding table. While eating, Seaton watched the engine —when he was not watching Dorothy—and talked to her. Crane and Margaret chatted easily. DuQuesne, except when addressed directly, maintained a self-sufficient silence.

After another observation Seaton said, "DuQuesne, we're almost five thousand light-years away from Earth, and getting farther away at about one light-year per minute."

"It'd be poor technique to ask how you know?"

"It would. Those figures are right. But we've got only four bars of copper left. Enough to stop us and some to spare, but not nearly enough to get us back, even by drifting —too many lifetimes on the way."

"So we land somewhere and dig us some copper."

"Check. What I wanted to ask you—isn't a copper-bearing sun apt to have copper-bearing planets?"

"I'd say so."

"Then take the spectroscope, will you, and pick out a sun somewhere up ahead—down ahead, I mean—for us to shoot at? And Mart, I s'pose we'd better take our regular twelve-hour tricks—no, eight; we've got to either trust the guy or kill him—I'll take the first watch. Beat it to bed."

"Not so fast." Crane said. "If I remember correctly, it's my turn."

"Ancient history doesn't count. I'll flip you a nickle for it. Heads, I win."

Seaton won, and the worn-out travelers went to their rooms—all except Dorothy, who lingered to bid her lover a more intimate good-night.

Seated beside him, his arm around her and her head on his shoulder, she sat blissfully until she noticed, for the first time, her bare left hand. She caught her breath and her eyes grew round.

" 'Smatter, Red?"

"Oh, Dick!" she exclaimed in dismay, "I simply forgot everything about taking what was left of my ring out of the doctor's engine!"

"Huh? What are you talking about?"

She told him; and he told her about Martin and himself.

"Oh, Dick—Dick—it's so wonderful to be with you again!" she concluded. "I lived as many years as we covered miles!"

"It was tough . . . you had it a lot worse than we did . . . but it makes me ashamed all over to think of the way I blew my stack at Wilson's. If it hadn't been for Martin's cautious old bean we'd've . . . we owe him a lot, Dimples."

"Yes, we do . . . but don't worry about the debt, Dick. Just don't ever let slip a word to Peggy about Martin being rich, is all."

"Oh, a matchmaker now? But why not? She wouldn't think any less of him—that's one reason I'm marrying you, you know—for your money."

Dorothy snickered sunnily. "I know. But listen, you poor, dumb, fortune-hunting darling—if Peggy had any idea that Martin is the one and only M. Reynolds Crane she'd curl right up into a ball. She'd think he'd think she was chasing him and then he *would* think so. As it is, he acts perfectly natural. He hasn't talked that way to any girl except me for five years, and he wouldn't talk to me until he found out for sure I wasn't out after him."

"Could be, pet," Seaton agreed. "On one thing you really chirped it—he's been shot at so much he's wilder than a hawk!"

At the end of eight hours Crane took over and Seaton stumbled to his room, where he slept for over ten hours like a man in a trance. Then, rising, he exercised and went out into the saloon.

Dorothy, Peggy and Crane were at breakfast; Seaton joined them. They ate the gayest, most carefree meal they had had since leaving earth. Some of the worst bruises still showed a little, but, under the influence of the potent if painful amylophene, all soreness, stiffness, and pain had disappeared.

After they had finished eating, Seaton said, "You suggested, Mart, that those gyroscope bearings may have been stressed beyond the yield-point. I'll take an integrating goniometer . . ."

"Break that down to our size, Dick—Peggy's and mine," Dorothy said.

"Can do. Take some tools and see if anything got bent out of shape back there. It might be an idea, Dot, to come along and hold my head while I think."

"That *is* an idea—if you never have another one."

Crane and Margaret went over and sat down at one of the crystal-clear ports. She told him her story frankly and fully, shuddering with horror as she recalled the awful, helpless fall during which Perkins had been killed.

"We have a heavy score to settle with that Steel crowd and with DuQuesne," Crane said, slowly. "We can convict him of abduction now. . . . Perkin's death wasn't murder, then?"

"Oh, no. He was just like a mad animal. He had to kill him. But the doctor, as they call him, is just as bad. He's so utterly heartless and ruthless, so cold and scientific, it gives me the compound shivers, just to think about him."

"And yet Dorothy said he saved her life?"

"He did, from Perkins; but that was just as strictly pragmatic as everything else he has ever done. He wanted her alive: dead, she wouldn't have been any use to him. He's as nearly a robot as any human being can be, that's what I think."

"I'm inclined to agree with you. . . . Nothing would please Dick better than a good excuse for killing him."

"He isn't the only one. And the way he ignores what we all feel shows what a machine he is. . . . What's that?" The *Skylark* had lurched slightly.

"Just a swing around a star, probably." He looked at the board, then led her to a lower port. "We are passing the star Dick was heading for, far too fast to stop. DuQuesne will pick out another. See that planet over there"—he pointed —"and that smaller one, there?"

She saw the two planets—one like a small moon, the other much smaller—and watched the sun increase rapidly in size as the *Skylark* flew on at such a pace that any earthly distance would have been covered as soon as it was begun. So appalling was their velocity that the ship was bathed in the light of that strange sun only for moments, then was surrounded again by darkness.

Their seventy-two-hour flight without a pilot had seemed a miracle; now it seemed entirely possible that they could fly in a straight line for weeks without encountering any obstacle, so vast was the emptiness in comparison with the points of light scattered about in it. Now and then they passed closely enough to a star so that it seemed to move fairly rapidly; but for the most part the stars stood, like distant mountain peaks to travelers in a train, in the same position for many minutes.

Awed by the immensity of the universe, the two at the window were silent, not with the silence of embarrassment but with that of two friends in the presence of a thing far beyond the reach of words. As they stared out into infinity, each felt as never before the pitiful smallness of the whole world they had known, and the insignificance of human beings and their works. Silently their minds reached out to each other in understanding.

Unconsciously Margaret half shuddered and moved closer

to Crane; and a tender look came over Crane's face as he looked down at the beautiful young woman at his side. For she was beautiful. Rest and food had erased the marks of her imprisonment. Dorothy's deep and unassumed faith in the ability of Seaton and Crane had quieted her fears. And finally, a costume of Dorothy's well-made—and exceedingly expensive!—clothes, which fitted her very well and in which she looked her best and knew it, had completely restored her self-possession.

He looked up quickly and again studied the stars; but now, in addition to the wonders of space, he saw a mass of wavy black hair, high-piled upon a queenly head; deep brown eyes veiled by long, black lashes; sweet, sensitive lips; a firmly rounded, dimpled chin; and a beautifully formed young body.

"How stupendous . . . how unbelievably great this is. . . ." Margaret whispered. "How vastly greater than any perception one could possibly get on Earth . . . and yet . . ."

She paused, with her lip caught under two white teeth, then went on, hesitatingly, "But doesn't it seem to you, Mr. Crane, that there is something in man as great as even all this? That there must be, or Dorothy and I could not be sailing out here in such a wonderful thing as this *Skylark*, which you and Dick Seaton have made?"

Days passed. Dorothy timed her waking hours with those of Seaton—preparing his meals and lightening the tedium of his long vigils at the board—and Margaret did the same thing for Crane. But often they assembled in the saloon, while DuQuesne was on watch, and there was much fun and laughter, as well as serious discussion, among the four. Margaret, already adopted as a friend, proved a delightful companion. Her ready tongue, her quick, delicate wit, and her facility of expression delighted all three.

One day Crane suggested to Seaton that they should take notes, in addition to the photographs they had been taking.

"I know comparatively little of astronomy, but, with the instruments we have, we should be able to get data, especially on planetary systems, which would be of interest to astronomers. Miss Spencer, being a secretary, could help us?"

"Sure," Seaton said. "That's an idea—nobody else ever had a chance to do it before."

"I'll be glad to—taking notes is the best thing I do!" Margaret cried, and called for pad and pencils.

After that, the two worked together for several hours on each of Martin's off shifts.

The *Skylark* passed one solar system after another, with a velocity so great that it was impossible to land. Margaret's association with Crane, begun as a duty, became a very real pleasure for them both. Working together in research, sitting together at the board in easy conversation or in equally easy silence, they compressed into days more real companionship than is usually possible in months.

Oftener and oftener, as time went on, Crane found the vision of his dream home floating in his mind as he steered the *Skylark* in her meteoric flight or as he lay strapped into his narrow bunk. Now, however, the central figure of the vision, instead of being a blur, was clear and sharply defined. And for her part, Margaret was drawn more and more to the quiet and unassuming, but steadfast young inventor, with his wide knowledge and his keen, incisive mind.

The *Skylark* finally slowed down enough to make a landing possible, and course was laid toward the nearest planet of a copper-bearing sun. As vessel neared planet a wave of excitement swept through four of the five. They watched the globe grow larger, glowing white, its outline softened by the atmosphere surrounding it. It had two satellites; its sun, a great, blazing orb, looked so big and so hot that Margaret became uneasy.

"Isn't it dangerous to get so close, Dick?"

"Uh-uh. Watching the pyrometers is part of the pilot's job. Any overheating and he'd snatch us away in a hurry."

They dropped into the atmosphere and on down, almost to the surface. The air was breatheable, its composition being very similar to that of Earth's air, except that the carbon dioxide was substantially higher. Its pressure was somewhat high, but not too much; its temperature, while high, was endurable. The planet's gravitational pull was about ten per cent higher than Earth's. The ground was almost hidden by a rank growth of vegetation, but here and there appeared glade-like openings.

Landing upon one of the open spaces, they found the ground solid and stepped out. What appeared to be a glade was in reality a rock; or rather a ledge of apparently solid metal, with scarcely a loose fragment to be seen. At one end of the ledge rose a giant tree, wonderfully symmetrical, but of a peculiar form, its branches being longer at the top than at the bottom and having broad, dark-green leaves, long thorns, and odd, flexible, shoot-like tendrils. It stood as an outpost of the dense vegetation beyond. The fern-trees, towering two hundred feet or more into the air were totally unlike the forests of Earth. They were an intensely vivid green and stood motionless in the still, hot air. Not a sign of animal life was to be seen; the whole landscape seemd to be asleep.

"A younger planet than ours," DuQuesne said. "In the Carboniferous, or about. Aren't those fern-trees like those in the coal measures, Seaton?"

"Check—I was just trying to think what they reminded me of. But it's this ledge that interests me no end. Who ever heard of a chunk of noble metal this big?"

"How do you know it's noble?" Dorothy asked.

"No corrosion, and its probably been sitting here for a million years." Seaton, who had walked over to one of the loose lumps, kicked it with his heavy shoe. It did not move.

He bent over to pick it up, with one hand. It still did not move. With both hands and all the strength of his back he could lift it, but that was all.

"What do you make of this, DuQuesne?"

DuQuesne lifted the mass, then took out his knife and scraped. He studied the freshly-exposed metal and the scrapings, then scraped and studied again.

"Hmm. Platinum group, almost certainly . . . and the only known member of that group with that peculiar bluish sheen is your X."

"But didn't we agree that free X and copper couldn't exist on the same planet, and that planets of copper-bearing suns carry copper?"

"Yes, but that doesn't make it true. If this stuff is X, it'll give the cosmologists something to fight about for the next twenty years. I'll take these scrapings and run a couple of quickies."

"Do that, and I'll gather in these loose nuggets. If it's X —and I'm pretty sure it mostly is—that'll be enough to run all the power-plants of Earth for ten thousand years."

Crane and Seaton, accompanied by the two girls, rolled the nearer pieces of metal up to the ship. Then, as the quest led them farther and farther afield, Crane protested.

"This is none too safe, Dick."

"It looks perfectly safe to me. Quiet as a—"

Margaret screamed. Her head was turned, looking backward at the *Skylark*; her face was a mask of horror.

Seaton drew his pistol as he whirled, only to check his finger on the trigger and lower his hand. "Nothing but X-plosive bullets," he said, and the four watched a thing come out slowly from behind their ship.

Its four huge, squat legs supported a body at least a hun-

"*—Mighty mandibles against poisonous sting,
the furious battle raged.*"

dred feet long, pursy and ungainly; at the end of a long, sinuous neck a small head seemed composed entirely of cavernous mouth armed with row upon row of carnivorous teeth. Dorothy gasped with terror; both girls shrank closer to the two men, who maintained a baffled silence as the huge beast slid its hideous head along the hull of the vessel.

"I can't shoot, Mart—it'd wreck the boat—and if I had any solids they wouldn't be any good."

"No. We had better hide until it goes away. You two take that ledge, we'll take this one."

"Or gets far enough away from the Skylark so we can blow him apart," Seaton added as, with Dorothy close beside him, he dropped behind the low bulwark.

Margaret, her staring eyes fixed upon the monster, remained motionless until Crane touched her gently and drew her down to his side. "Don't be frightened, Peggy. It will go away soon."

"I'm not, now—much." She drew a deep breath. "If you weren't here, though, Martin, I'd be dead of pure fright."

His arm tightened around her; then he forced it to relax. This was neither the time nor the place. . . .

A roll of gunfire came from the Skylark. The creature roared in pain and rage, but was quickly silenced by the stream of .50-caliber machine-gun bullets.

"DuQuesne's on the job—let's go!" Seaton cried, and the four rushed up the slope. Making a detour to avoid the writhing body, they plunged through the opening door. DuQuesne closed the lock. They huddled together in overwhelming relief as an appalling tumult arose outside.

The scene, so quiet a few moments before, was horribly changed. The air seemed filled with hideous monsters. Winged lizards of prodigious size hurtled through the air to crash against the Skylark's armored hull. Flying monstrosities, with the fangs of tigers, attacked viciously. Dorothy screamed and started back as a scorpion-like thing ten feet in length leaped at the window in front of her, its terrible sting spraying the quartz with venom. As it fell to the ground a spider—if an eight-legged creature with spines instead of hair, faceted eyes, and a bloated, globular body weighing hundreds of pounds may be called a spider—leaped upon it; and, mighty mandibles against terrible sting, a furious battle raged. Twelve-foot cockroaches climbed nimbly across the fallen timber of the morass and began feeding voraciously on the carcass of the creature DuQuesne had killed. They were promptly driven away by another animal, a living nightmare of that reptilian age which apparently combined the nature and disposition of *tyrannosaurus rex* with a physical shape approximating that of the saber-tooth tiger. This newcomer towered fifteen feet high at the shoulders and had a mouth disproportionate even to his great size; a mouth armed with sharp fangs three feet in length. He had barely begun his meal, however, when he was challeneged by another nightmare, a thing shaped more or less like a crocodile.

The crocodile charged. The tiger met him head on, fangs front and rending claws outstretched. Clawing, striking, tearing savagely, an avalanche of bloodthirsty rage, the combatants stormed up and down the little island.

Suddenly the great tree bent over and lashed out against both animals. It transfixed them with its thorns, which the watchers now saw were both needle-pointed and barbed. It ripped at them with its long branches, which were in fact highly lethal spears. The broad leaves, equipped with sucking disks, wrapped themselves around the hopelessly impaled victims. The long, slender twigs or tendrils, each of which now had an eye at its extremity, waved about at a safe distance.

After absorbing all of the two gladiators that was absorbable, the tree resumed its former position, motionless in all its strange, outlandish beauty.

Dorothy licked her lips, which were almost as white as her face. "I think I'm going to be sick," she remarked, conversationally.

"No you aren't." Seaton tightened his arm. "Chin up, ace."

"Okay, chief. Maybe not—this time.' Color began to reappear on her cheeks. "But Dick, will you please blow up that horrible tree? It wouldn't be so bad if it were ugly, like the rest of the things, but it's so beautiful!"

"I sure will. I think we'd better get out of here. This is no place to start a copper mine, even if there's any copper here, which there probably isn't. . . . It is X, DuQuesne, isn't it?"

"Yes. Ninety-nine plus per cent, at least."

"That reminds me." Seaton turned to DuQuesne, hand outstretched. "You squared it, Blackie. Say the word and the war's all off."

DuQuesne ignored the hand. "Not on my side," he said, evenly. "I act as one of the party as long as I'm with you. When we get back, however, I still intend to take both of you out of circulation." He went to his room.

"Well, I'll be a . . ." Seaton bit off a word. "He ain't a man—he's a cold-blooded fish!"

"He's a machine—a robot." Margaret declared. "I always thought so, and now I know it!"

"We'll pull his cork when we get back," Seaton said. "He asked for it—we'll give him both barrels!"

Crane went to the board, and soon they were approaching another planet, which was surrounded by a dense fog. Descending slowly, they found it to be a mass of boiling-hot steam and rank vapor, under enormous pressure.

The next planet looked barren and dead. Its atmosphere was clear, but of a peculiar yellowish-green color. Analysis showed over ninety per cent chlorine. No life of any Earthly type could exist naturally upon such a world and a search for copper, even in space-suits, would be extremely difficult if not impossible.

"Well," Seaton said, as they were once more in space, "We've got copper enough to visit quite a few more solar systems if we have to. But there's a nice, hopeful-looking planet right over there. It may be the one we're looking for."

Arriving in the belt of atmosphere, they tested it as before and found it satisfactory.

chapter **15**

THEY DESCENDED RAPIDLY, OVER A LARGE city set in the middle of a vast, level, beautifully planted plain. As they watched, the city vanished and became a mountain summit, with valleys falling away on all sides as far as the eye could reach.

"Huh! I never saw a mirage like *that* before!" Seaton exclaimed. "But we'll land, if we finally have to swim!"

The ship landed gently upon the summit, its occupants more than half expecting the mountain to disappear beneath them. Nothing happened, however, and the five clustered in the lock, wondering whether or not to disembark. They could see no sign of life; but each felt the presence of a vast, invisible something.

Suddenly a man materialized in the air before them; a man identical with Seaton in every detail, down to the smudge of grease under one eye and the exact design of his Hawaiian sport shirt.

"Hello, folks," he said, in Seaton's tone and style. "S'prised that I know your language—huh, you would be. Don't even understand telepathy, or the ether, or the relationship between time and space. Not even the fourth dimension."

Changing instantaneously from Seaton's form to Dorothy's, the stranger went on without a break. "Electrons and neutrons and things—nothing here, either."

The form became DuQuesne's. "Ah, a freer type, but blind, dull, stupid; another nothing. As Martin Crane; the same. As Peggy, still the same, as was of course to be expected. Since you are all nothings in essence, of a race so low in the scale that it will be millions of years before it will rise even above death and death's clumsy attendant necessity, sex, it is of course necessary for me to make of you nothings in fact: to dematerialize you."

In Seaton's form the being stared at Seaton, who felt his senses reel under the impact of an awful, if insubstantial, blow. Seaton fought back with all his mind and remained standing.

"What's this?" the stranger exclaimed in surprise. "This is the first time in millions of cycles that mere matter, which is only a manifestation of mind, has refused to obey a mind of power. There's something screwy somewhere." He switched to Crane's shape.

"Ah, I am not a perfect reproduction—there is some subtle difference. The external form is the same; the internal structure likewise. The molecules of substance are arranged properly, as are the atoms in the molecules. The electrons, neutrons, protons, positrons, neutrinos, mesons . . . nothing amiss on that level. On the third level . . ."

"Let's go!" Seaton exclaimed, drawing Dorothy backward and reaching for the airlock switch. "This dematerialization stuff may be pie for him, but believe me, it's none of my dish."

"No, no!" the stranger remonstrated, "You really must stay and be dematerialized—alive or dead."

He drew his pistol. Being in Crane's form, he drew slowly, as Crane did; and Seaton's Mark I shell struck him before the pistol cleared his pocket. The pseudo-body was volatilized; but, just to make sure, Crane fired a Mark V into the ground through the last open chink of the closing lock.

Seaton leaped to the board. As he did so, a creature materialized in the air in front of him—and crashed to the floor as he threw on the power. It was a frightful thing—

"It was a frightful thing, like nothing ever before seen upon any world; with great teeth, long, sharp claws, and an automatic pistol clutched firmly in a human hand."

outrageous teeth, long claws, and an automatic pistol held in a human hand. Forced flat by the fierce acceleration, it was unable to lift either itself or the weapon.

"We take one trick!' Seaton blazed. "Stick to matter and I'll run along with you 'til my ankles catch fire!"

"That is a childish defiance. It speaks well for your courage, but not for your intelligence," the animal said, and vanished.

A moment later Seaton's hair stood on end as a pistol appeared upon his board, clamped to it by bands of steel. The slide jerked; the trigger moved; the hammer came down. However, there was no explosion, but merely a click. Seaton, paralyzed by the rapid succession of stunning events, was surprised to find himself still alive.

"Oh, I was almost sure it wouldn't explode," the gun-barrel said, chattily, in a harsh, metallic voice. "You see, I haven't derived the formula of your sub-nuclear structure yet, hence I could not make an actual explosive. By the use of crude force I could kill you in any one of many different ways. . . ."

"Name one!" Seaton snapped.

"Two, if you like. I could materialize as five masses of metal directly over your heads, and fall. I could, by a sufficient concentration of effort, materialize a sun in your immediate path. Either method would succeed, would it not?"

"I . . . I guess it would," Seaton admitted, grudgingly.

"But such crude work is distasteful in the extreme, and is never, under any conditions, mandatory. Furthermore, you are not quite the complete nothings that my first rough analysis seemed to indicate. In particular, the DuQuesne of you has the rudiments of a quality which, while it cannot be called mental ability, may in time develop into a quality which may just possibly make him assimilable into the purely intellectual stratum.

"Furthermore, you have given me a notable and entirely unexpected amount of exercise and enjoyment and can be made to give me more—much more—as follows: I will spend the next sixty of your minutes at work upon that formula—your sub-nuclear structure. Its derivation is comparatively simple, requiring only the solution of ninety-seven simultaneous differential equations and an integration in ninety-seven dimensions. If you can interfere with my computations sufficiently to prevent me from deriving that formula within the stipulated period of time you may return to your fellow nothings exactly as you now are. The first minute begins when the sweep-hand of your chronometer touches zero; that is . . . now."

Seaton cut the power to one gravity and sat up, eyes closed tight and frowning in the intensity of his mental effort.

"You can't do it, you immaterial lug!" he thought, savagely. "There are too many variables. No mind, however inhuman, can handle more than ninety-one differentials at once . . . you're wrong; that's theta, not epsilon. . . . It's X, not Y or Z. Alpha! Beta! Ha, there's a slip; a bad one—got to go back and start all over. . . . Nobody can integrate above ninety-six brackets . . . no body and no thing or mind in this whole, entire, cock-eyed universe! . . ."

Seaton cast aside any thought of the horror of their position. He denied any feeling of suspense. He refused to consider the fact that both he and his beloved Dorothy might at any instant be hurled into nothingness. Closing his mind deliberately to everything else, he fought that weirdly inimical entity with everything he had: with all his single-mindedness of purpose; with all his power of concentration; with all the massed and directed strength of his keen, highly-trained brain.

The hour passed.

"You win," the gun-barrel said. "More particularly, I should say that the DuQuesne of you won. To my surprise and delight that one developed his nascent quality very markedly during this short hour. Keep on going as you have been going, my potential kinsman; keep on studying under those eastern masters as you have been studying; and it is within the realm of possibility that, even in your short lifetime, you may become capable of withstanding the stresses concomitant with induction into our ranks."

The pistol vanished. So did the planet behind them. The enveloping, pervading field of mental force disappeared. All five knew surely, without any trace of doubt, that that entity, whatever it had been, had gone.

"Did all that really happen, Dick?" Dorothy asked, tremulously, "or have I been having the great-great-grandfather of all nightmares?"

"It hap . . . . that is, I guess it happened . . . or maybe . . . Mart, if you could code that and shove it into a mechanical brain, what answer do you think would come out?"

"I don't know. I—simply—do—not—know." Crane's

mind, the mind of a highly-trained engineer, rebelled. No part of this whole fantastic episode could be explained by anything he knew. None of it could possibly have happened. Nevertheless . . .

"Either it happened or we were hypnotized. If so, who was the hypnotist, and where? Above all, why? It must have happened, Dick."

"I'll buy that, wild as it sounds. Now, DuQuesne, how about you?"

"It happened. I don't know how or why it did, but I believe that it did. I've quit denying the impossibility of anything. If I had believed that your steam-bath flew out of the window by itself, that day, none of us would be out here now."

"If it happened, you were apparently the prime operator in saving our bacon. Who in blazes are those eastern masters you've been studying under, and what did you study?"

"I don't know." He lit a cigarette, took two deep inhalations. "I wish I did. I've studied several esoteric philosophies . . . perhaps I can find out which one it was. I'll certainly try . . . for that, gentlemen, would be my idea of heaven." He left the room.

It took some time for the four to recover from the shock of that encounter. In fact, they had not yet fully recovered from it when Crane found a close cluster of stars, each emitting a peculiar greenish light which, in the spectroscope, blazed with copper lines. When they had approached so close that the suns were widely spaced in the heavens Crane asked Seaton to take his place at the board while he and Margaret tried to locate a planet.

They went down to the observatory, but found that they were still too far away and began taking notes. Crane's mind was not upon his work, however, but was filled with thoughts of the girl at his side. The intervals between comments became longer and longer, until the two were standing in silence.

The *Skylark* lurched a little, as she had done hundreds of times before. As usual, Crane put out a steadying arm. This time, however, in that highly charged atmosphere, the gesture took on a new significance. Both blushed hotly; and, as their eyes met, each saw what they had both wanted most to see.

Slowly, almost as though without volition, Crane put his other arm around her. A wave of deeper crimson flooded her face; but her lips lifted to his and her arms went up around his neck.

"Margaret—Peggy—I had intended to wait—but why should we wait? You know how much I love you, my dearest!"

"I think I do . . . I know I do . . . my Martin!"

Presently they made their way back to the engine-room, hoping that their singing joy was inaudible, their new status invisible. They might have kept their secret for a time had not Seaton promptly asked, "What did you find, Mart?"

The always self-possessed Crane looked panicky; Margaret's fair face glowed a deeper and deeper pink.

"Yes, what did you find?" Dorothy demanded, with a sudden, vivid smile of understanding.

"My future wife," Crane answered, steadily.

The two girls hugged each other and the two men gripped hands, each of the four knowing that in these two unions there was nothing whatever of passing fancy.

A planet was located and the Skylark flew toward it.

"It's pretty deep in, Mart. DuQuesne and I haven't got enough dope yet to plot this mess of suns, so we don't know exactly where any of them really are, but that planet's somewhere down in the middle. Would that make any difference?"

"No. There are many closer ones, but they are too big or too small or lack water or atmosphere or have some other drawback. Go ahead."

When they neared atmosphere and cut the drive, there were seventeen great suns, scattered in all directions in the sky.

"Air-pressure at the surface, thirty pounds per square inch. Composition, approximately normal except for three-tenths of one per cent of a fragrant, non-poisonous gas with which I am not familiar. Temperature, one hundred degrees Fahrenheit. Surface gravity, four-tenths Earth," came the various reports.

Seaton let the vessel settle slowly toward the ocean beneath them; the water was an intensely deep blue. He took a sample, ran it through the machine, and yelled.

"Ammoniacal copper sulphate! Hot dog! Let's go!" Seaton laid a course toward the nearest continent.

chapter 16

AS THE SKYLARK APPROACHED THE SHORE ITS
occupants heard a rapid succession of detonations, apparently coming from the direction in which they were traveling.

"Wonder what that racket is," Seaton said. "Sounds like
big guns and high explosive—not atomic, though."

"Check." DuQuesne said. "Even allowing for the density
of this air, that kind of noise is not made by pop-guns."

Seaton closed the lock to keep out the noise, and advanced the speed lever until the vessel tilted sharply under
the pull of the engine.

"Go easy, Seaton," DuQuesne cautioned. "We don't
want to stop one of their shells—they may not be like ours."

"Easy it is. I'll stay high."

As the *Skylark* closed up, the sound grew heavier and
clearer. It was one practically continuous explosion.

"There they are," said Seaton, who, from his board,
could scan the whole field of vision. "From port six, five
o'clock low."

While the other four were making their way to the indicated viewpoint Seaton went on. "Aerial battleships, eight
of 'em. Four are about the shape of ours—no wings, act
like 'copters—but I never saw anything like the other four."

Neither had either Crane or DuQuesne.

"They must be animals," Crane decided, finally. "I do
not believe that any engineer, anywhere, would design
machines like that."

Four of the contestants were animals. Here indeed was
a new kind of animal—an animal able and eager to engage
a first-class battleship.

Each had an enormous, torpedo-shaped body, with scores
of long tentacles and a dozen or so immense wings. Each
had a row of eyes along each side and a sharp, prow-like
beak. Each was covered with scale-like plates of transparent
armor; wings and tentacles were made of the same substance.

That it was real and highly effective armor there was no
doubt, for each battleship bristled with guns and each gun

was putting out an almost continuous stream of fire. Shells bursting against the creatures filled the region with flame and haze, and produced an uninterrupted roll of sound appalling in its intensity.

In spite of that desperate concentration of fire, however, the animals went straight in. Beaks tore yards-wide openings in hulls; flailing wings smashed superstructures flat; writhing, searching tentacles wrenched guns from their mounts and seized personnel. Out of action, one battleship was held while tentacles sought out and snatched its crew. Then it was dropped, to crash some twenty thousand feet below. One animal was blown apart. Two more battleships and two more animals went down.

The remaining battleship was half wrecked; the animal was as good as new. Thus the final duel did not last long.

The monster darted away after something, which the observers in the *Skylark* saw for the first time—a fleet of small airships in full flight away from the scene of battle. Fast as they were, the animal was covering three miles to their one.

"We can't stand for anything like that!" Seaton cried, as he threw on power and the *Skylark* leaped ahead. "When I yank him away, Mart, sock him with a Mark Ten!"

The monster seized the largest, most gaily decorated plane just as the *Skylark* came within sighting distance. In four almost simultaneous motions Seaton focused the attractor on the huge beak of the thing, shoved on its power, pointed the engine straight up and give it five notches.

There was a crash of rending metal as the monster was torn loose from its prey. Seaton hauled it straight up for a hundred miles, while it struggled so savagely in that invisible and incomprehensible grip that the thousands of tons of mass of the *Skylark* tossed and pitched like a rowboat in a storm at sea.

Crane fired. There was a blare of sound that paralyzed their senses, even inside the vessel and in the thin air of that enormous elevation. There was a furiously-boiling, furiously-expanding ball of . . . of what? The detonation of a Mark Ten load cannot be described. It must be seen; and even then, it cannot be understood. It can scarcely be believed.

No bit large enough to be seen remained of that mass of almost indestructible armor.

Seaton reversed the bar and drove straight down, catching the crippled flagship at about five thousand feet. He focused the attractor and lowered the plane gently to the ground. The other airships, which had been clustering around their leader in near-suicidal attempts at rescue, landed nearby.

As the Skylark landed beside he wrecked plane, the Earthmen saw that it was surrounded by a crowd of people—men and women identical in form and feature with themselves. They were a superbly-molded race. The men were almost as big as Seaton and DuQuesne; the women were noticeably taller than the two Earth-women. The men wore collars of metal, numerous metallic ornaments, and heavily-jeweled belts and shoulder-straps which were hung with weapons. The women were not armed, but were even more highly decorated than the men. They fairly scintillated with jewels.

The natives wore no clothing, and their smooth skins shone a dark, livid, utterly strange color in the yellowish-bluish-green glare of the light. Their skins were green, undoubtedly; but it was no green known to Earth. The "whites" of their eyes were a light yellowish-green. The heavy hair of the women and the close-cropped locks of the men were a very dark green—almost black—as were also their eyes.

"What a color." Seaton said, wonderingly. "They're human, I guess . . . except for the color . . . but Great Cat, what a color!"

"How much of that is pigment and how much is due to this light is a question," said Crane. "If we were outside, away from our daylight lamps, we might look like that, too."

"Horrors, I hope not!" Dorothy exclaimed. "If I'm going to I won't take a step out of this ship, so there!"

"Sure you will," Seaton said. "You'll look like a choice piece of modern art and your hair will be jet black. Come on and give the natives a treat."

"Then what color will mine be?" Margaret asked.

"I'm not quite sure. Probably a very dark and very beautiful green," he grinned gleefully. "My hunch is that this is going to be some visit. Wait 'til I get a couple of props . . . Shall we go? Come on, Dot."

"Roger. I'll try anything, once."

"Margaret?"

"Onward, men of Earth!"

Seaton opened the lock and the five stood in the chamber, looking at the throng outside. Seaton raised both arms above his head, in what he hoped was the universal sign of peaceful intent. In response a man of Herculean build, so splendidly decorated that his harness was one gleaming mass of jewels, waved one arm and shouted a command. The crowd promptly fell back, leaving a clear space of a hundred yards. The man unbuckled his harness, let everything drop, and advanced naked toward the *Skylark*, both arms aloft in Seaton's own gesture.

Seaton started down.

"No, Dick, talk to him from here," Crane advised.

"Nix." Seaton said. "What he can do, I can. Except undress in mixed company. He won't know that I've got a gun in my pocket, and it won't take me more than half an hour to pull it if I have to."

"Go on, then. DuQuesne and I will come along."

"Double nix. He's alone, so I've got to be. Some of his boys are covering the field, though, so you might draw your gats and hold them so they show."

Seaton stepped down and went to meet the stranger. When they had approached to within a few feet of each other the stranger stopped, stood erect, flexed his left arm smartly, so that the finger-tips touched his left ear, and smiled broadly, exposing clean, shining, green teeth. He spoke—a meaningless jumble of sound. His voice, coming from so big a man, seemed light and thin.

Seaton smiled in return and saluted as the other had done.

"Hail and greetings, Oh High Panjandrum," Seaton said, cordially, his deep voice fairly booming out in the dense, heavy air. "I get the drift, and I'm glad you're peaceable; I wish I could tell you so."

The native tapped himself upon the chest. "Nalboon," he said, distinctly and impressively.

"Nalboon," Seaton repeated; then said, in the other's tone and manner, while pointing to himself, "Seaton."

"See Tin," Nalboon said, and smiled again. Again indicating himself, he said, "Domak gok Mardonale."

That was evidently a title, so Seaton had to give himself one. "Boss of the Road," he said, drawing himself up with pride.

Thus properly introduced to his visitor, Nalboon pointed to the crippled plane, inclined his royal head slightly in thanks or in acknowledgment of the service rendered— Seaton could not tell which—then turned to face his people with one arm upraised. He shouted an order in which

Seaton could distinguish something that sounded like "See Tin Basz Uvvy Roagd."

Instantly every right arm in the crowd was aloft, that of each man bearing a weapon, while the left arms snapped into that peculiar salute. A mighty cry arose as all repeated the name and title of the distinguished visitor.

Seaton turned. "Bring out one of those big four-color signal rockets, Mart!" he called. "We've got to acknowledge a reception like this!"

The party appeared, DuQuesne carrying the rocket with an exaggerated deference. Seaton shrugged one shoulder and a cigarette-case appeared in his hand. Nalboon started and, in spite of his self-control, glanced at it in surprise. The case flew open and Seaton, after taking a cigarette, pointed to another.

"Smoke?" he asked, affably. Nalboon took one, but had no idea whatever of what to do with it. This astonishment at simple sleight-of-hand and ignorance of tobacco emboldened Seaton. Reaching into his mouth, he pulled out a flaming match—at which Nalboon jumped straight backward at least a foot. Then, while Nalboon and his people watched in straining attention, Seaton lit the weed, halfconsumed it in two long drags, swallowed the half, regurgitated it still alight, took another puff, and swallowed the butt.

"I'm good, I admit, but not that good," Seaton said to Crane. "I never laid 'em in the aisles like that before. This rocket'll tie 'em up like pretzels. Keep clear, everybody."

He bowed deeply to Nalboon, pulling a lighted match from his ear as he did so, and lighted the fuse. There was a roar, a shower of sparks, a blaze of colored fire as the rocket flew upward; but, to Seaton's surprise, Nalboon took it quite as a matter of course, merely saluting gravely in acknowledgment of the courtesy.

Seaton motioned his party to come up and turned to Crane.

"Better not, Dick. Let him keep on thinking that one Boss is all there is."

"Not by a long shot. There's only one of him—two of us bosses would be twice as good." He introduced Crane, with great ceremony, as "Boss of the Skylark", whereupon the grand salute of the people was repeated.

Nalboon gave an order, and a squad of soldiers brought up a group of people, apparently prisoners. Seven men and seven women, they were of a much lighter color than the natives. They were naked, except for jeweled collars worn by all and a thick metal belt worn by one of the men. They all walked proudly, scorn for their captors in every step.

Nalboon barked an order. Thirteen of the prisoners stared back at him, motionlessly defiant. The man wearing the belt, who had been studying Seaton closely, said something, whereupon they all prostrated themselves. Nalboon waved his hand—giving the group to Seaton and Crane. They accepted the gift with due thanks and the slaves placed themselves behind their new masters.

Seaton and Crane then tried to make Nalboon understand that they wanted copper, but failed dismally. Finally Seaton led the native into the ship and showed him the remnant of the power bar, indicating its original size and giving informaion as to the number desired by counting to sixteen upon his fingers. Nalboon understood, and, going outside, pointed upward toward the largest of the eleven suns visible, and swung his arm four times in a rising-and-setting arc. He then invited the visitors to get into his plane, but Seaton refused. They would follow, he explained, in their own vessel.

As they entered the *Skylark*, the slaves followed.

"We don't want them aboard, Dick," Dorothy protested. "There are too many of them. Not that I'm exactly scared, but . . ."

"We've got to," Seaton decided. "We're stuck with 'em. And besides—when in Rome, you've got to be a Roman candle, you know."

Nalboon's newly-invested flagship led the way; the *Skylark* followed, a few hundred yards behind and above it.

"I don't get these folks at all," Seaton said, thoughtfully. "They've got next century's machines, but never heard of sleight-of-hand. Class Nine rockets are old stuff, but matches scare them. Funny."

"It is surprising enough that their physical shape is the same as ours," Crane said. "It would be altogether too much to expect that all the details of development would be parallel."

The fleet approached a large city and the visitors from Earth studied with interest this metropolis of an unknown world. The buildings were all of the same height, flat-topped, arranged in random squares, rectangles, and triangles. There were no streets, the spaces between the buildings being park-like areas.

All traffic was in the air. Flying vehicles darted in all

directions, but the confusion was only apparent, not real, each class and each direction having its own level.

The fleet descended toward an immense building just outside the city proper and all landed upon its roof except the flagship, which led the Skylark to a landing-dock nearby.

As they disembarked Seaton said, "Don't be surprised at anything I pull off—I'm a walking storehouse of all kinds of small junk."

Nalboon led the way into an elevator, which dropped to the ground floor. Gates opened, and through ranks of prostrate people the party went out into the palace grounds of the emperor of the great nation of Mardonale.

It was a scene of unearthly splendor. Every shade of their peculiar spectrum was there, in solid, liquid, and gas. Trees were of all colors, as were grasses and flowers along the walks. Fountains played streams of various and constantly-changing hues. The air was tinted and perfumed, swirling through metal arches in billows of ever-varying colors and scents. Colors and combinations of colors impossible to describe were upon every hand, fantastically beautiful in that strong, steady, peculiar light.

"Isn't this gorgeous, Dick?" Dorothy whispered. "But I wish I had a mirror—you look simply *awful*—what kind of a scarecrow am I?"

"You've been under a mercury arc? Like that, only worse. Your hair isn't as black as I thought it would be, there's some funny green in it. Your lips, though, are really black. Your teeth are green. . . ."

"Stop it! Green teeth and black lips! That's enough—and I don't want a mirror!"

Nalboon led the way into the palace proper and into a dining hall, where a table was ready. This room had many windows, each of which was festooned with sparkling, scintillating gems. The walls were hung with a cloth resembling spun glass or nylon, which fell to the floor in shimmering waves of color.

There was no woodwork whatever. Doors, panels, tables and chairs were made of metal. A closer inspection of one of the tapestries showed that it, too, was of metal, its threads numbering thousands to the inch. Of vivid but harmonious colors, of a strange and intricate design, it seemed to writhe as its colors changed with every variation in the color of the light.

"Oh . . . isn't that stuff just too perfectly gorgeous?"

Dorothy breathed. "I'd give *anything* for a dress made out of it."

"Order noted." Seaton said. "I'll pick up ten yards of it when we get the copper."

"We'd better watch the chow pretty close, Seaton," DuQuesne said, as Nalboon waved them to the table.

"You chirped it. Copper, arsenic, and so forth. Very little here we can eat much of, I'd say."

"The girls and I will wait for you two chemists to approve each dish, then," Crane said.

The guests sat down, the light-skinned slaves standing behind them, and servants brought in heaping trays of food. There were joints and cuts of many kinds of meat; birds and fish, raw and cooked in various ways; green, pink, brown, purple, black and near-white vegetables and fruits. Slaves handed the diners peculiar instruments—knives with razor edges, needle-pointed stilettos, and wide, flexible spatulas which evidently were to serve as both forks and spoons.

"I simply can't eat with these things!" Dorothy exclaimed.

"That's where my lumberjack training comes in handy," Seaton grinned. "I can eat with a spatula four times as fast as you can with a fork. But we'll fix that."

Reaching out, apparently into the girls' hair, he brought out forks and spoons, much to the surprise of the natives.

DuQuesne and Seaton waved away most of the proferred foods without discussion. Then, tasting cautiously and discussing fully, they approved a few of the others. The approval, however, was very strictly limited.

"These probably won't poison us too much," DuQuesne said, pointing out the selected few. "That is, if we don't eat much now and don't eat any of it again too soon. I don't like this one little bit, Seaton."

"You and me both," Seaton agreed. "I don't think there'll be any next time."

Nalboon took a bowl full of blue crystals, sprinkled his food liberally with the substance, and passed the bowl to Seaton.

"Copper sulphate," Seaton said. "Good thing they put it on at the table instead of the kitchen, or we couldn't eat a bite of anything."

Seaton, returning the bowl, reached behind him and came up with a pair of salt- and pepper-shakers which, after seasoning his own food with them, he passed to his host. Nalboon tasted the pepper cautiously, then smiled in delight and half-emptied the shaker onto his plate. He then sprinkled a few grains of salt into his palm, studied them closely with growing amazement, and after a few rapid sentences poured them into a dish held by an officer who had sprung to his side. The officer also studied the few small crystals, then carefully washed Nalboon's hand. Nalboon turned to Seaton, plainly asking for the salt-cellar.

"Sure, my ripe and old." In the same mysterious way he produced another set, which he handed to Crane.

The meal progressed merrily, with much sign-language conversation between the two parties, a little of which was understood. It was evident that Nalboon, usually stern and reticent, was in an unusually pleasant and jovial mood.

After the meal Nalboon bade them a courteous farewell; and they were escorted to a suite of five connecting rooms by the royal usher and a company of soldiers, who mounted guard outside the suite.

Gathered in one room, they discussed sleeping arrangements. The girls insisted that they would sleep together, and that the men should occupy the rooms on either side. As the girls turned away, four slaves followed.

"I don't want these people and I can't make them go away," she protested again. "Can't you do something, Dick?"

"I don't think so. I think we're stuck with 'em as long as we're here. Don't you think so, Mart?"

"Yes. And from what I have seen of this culture, I infer that they will be executed if we discard them."

"Huh? How do . . . could be. We keep 'em, then, Dot."

"Of course, in that case. You keep the men and we'll take the women."

"Hmmm." He turned to Crane, saying under his breath, "They don't want us sleeping in the same room with any of these gorgeous gals, huh? I wonder why?"

Seaton waved all the women into the girls' room; but they hung back. One of them ran up to the man wearing the belt and spoke rapidly as she threw her arms around his neck in a perfectly human gesture. He shook his head, pointing toward Seaton several times as he reassured her. He then led her tenderly into the girls' room and the other women followed. Crane and DuQuesne having gone to their rooms with their attendants, the man with the belt started to help Seaton take off his clothes.

Stripped, Seaton stretched vigorously, the muscles writhing and rippling under the skin of mighty arms and broad shoulders as he twisted about, working off the stiffness of comparative confinement. The slaves stared in amazement at the display of musculature and talked rapidly among themselves as they gathered up Seaton's discarded clothing. Their chief picked up a salt-shaker, a silver fork, and a few other items that had fallen from the garments, apparently asking permission to do something with them. Seaton nodded and turned to his bed. He heard a slight clank of arms in the hall and began to wonder. Going to the window, he saw that there were guards outside as well. Were they honored guests or prisoners?

Three of the slaves, at a word from their leader, threw themselves on the floor and slept; but he himself did not rest. Opening the apparently solid metal belt he took out a great number of small tools, many tiny instruments, and several spools of insulated wire. He then took the articles Seaton had given him, taking extreme pains not to spill a single crystal of salt, and set to work. As he worked, hour after hour, a strange, exceedingly complex device took form under his flying fingers.

chapter **17**

SEATON DID NOT SLEEP WELL. IT WAS TOO hot. He was glad after eight hours, to get up. No sooner had he started to shave, however, than one of the slaves touched his arm, motioning him into a reclining chair and showing him a keen blade, long and slightly curved. Seaton lay down and the slave shaved him with a rapidity and smoothness he had never before experienced, so wonderfully sharp was the peculiar razor. Then the barber began to shave his superior, with no preliminary treatment save rubbing his face with a perfumed oil.

"Hold on a minute," said Seaton, "Here's something that helps a lot. Soap." He lathered the face with his brush, and the man with the belt looked up in surprised pleasure as his stiff beard was swept away with no pulling at all.

Seaton called to the others and soon the party was assembled in his room. All were dressed very lightly because of the unrelieved and unvarying heat, which was constant at one hundred degrees. A gong sounded and one of the slaves opened the door, ushering in servants bearing a table, ready set. The Earthlings did not eat anything, deciding that they would rather wait an hour or so and then eat in the *Skylark*. Hence the slaves had a much better meal than they otherwise would have had.

During that meal, Seaton was very much surprised at hearing Dorothy carrying on a labored conversation with one of the women.

"I knew you were a language shark, Dottie, but I didn't s'pose you could pick one up in a day."

"Oh, I can't. Just a few words. I can understand very little of what they're trying to tell me."

The woman spoke rapidly to the man with the belt, who immediately asked Seaton's permission to speak to Dorothy. Running across to her, he bowed and poured out such a stream of words that she held up her hand to silence him.

"Go slower, please," she said, and added a couple of words in his own language.

There ensued a very strange conversation between the slave couple and Dorothy, with much talking between the man and the woman, both talking at once to Dorothy, and much use of signs and sketches. Dorothy finally turned to Seaton with a frown.

"I can't make out half of what he tried to tell me, and I'm guessing at part of that. He wants you to take him somewhere, another room of the palace here, I think. He wants to get something. I can't quite make out what it is, or whether it was his and they took it away from him, or whether it's something of theirs that he wants to steal. He can't go alone. Martin was right, any of them will be shot if they stir without us. And he says—I'm pretty sure of this part—when you get there don't let any guards come inside."

"What do you think, Mart? I'm inclined to string along with this bunch, at least part way. I don't like Nalboon's 'honor guard' setup a bit—it smells. Like overripefish."

Crane concurred. Seaton and his slave started for the door. Dorothy went along.

"Better stay back, Dottie. We won't be gone long."

"I will not go back," she said, for his ears alone. "On this damn world I'm not going to be away from you one minute more than I absolutely have to."

"Hokay, ace," he replied, in the same tone. "You'd be amazed to find out how little there is in that idea for me to squawk about."

Preceded by the man with the belt and followed by half a dozen other slaves, they went out into the hall. No opposition was made to their going; but half a company of armed guards fell in with them as an escort, most of them looking at Seaton with a mixture of reverence and fear. The slave led the way to a room in a distant wing of the palace and opened the door. As Seaton stepped into it he saw that it was an audience chamber or courtroom and that it was now empty.

The guards approached the door. Seaton waved them back. All retreated across the hall except the officer in charge, who refused to move. Seaton, the personification of offended dignity, stared haughtily at the offender, who returned the stare with interest and stepped forward, fully intending to be the first to enter the room. Seaton, with the flat of his right hand on the officer's chest, pushed him back roughly, forgetting that his strength, great upon Earth, would be gigantic upon this smaller world. The officer spun across the corridor, knocking down three of his men in his flight. Picking himself up, he drew his sword and rushed, while his men fled in panic to the extreme end of the corridor.

Seaton did not wait for him, but leaped to meet him. With his vastly superior agility he dodged the falling broadsword and drove his right fist into the fellow's throat, with all the strength of arm and shoulder and all the momentum of his body behind the blow. Bones broke audibly as the officer's head snapped back. The body went high in air, turned two complete somersaults, crashed against the far wall, and dropped to the floor.

At this outrage, some of the guards started to lift their peculiar guns. Dorothy screamed a warning. Seaton drew and fired in one incredibly fast motion, the Mark I load obliterating the clustered soldiers and demolishing that end of the palace.

In the meantime the slave had taken several pieces of apparatus from a cabinet and had placed them in his belt. Stopping only to observe for a few moments a small instrument which he clamped to the head of the dead man, he led the party back to the room they had left and set to work upon the device he had built during the sleeping period. He connected it, in an extremely intricate network of wiring, with the pieces of apparatus he had just obtained.

"Whatever that is, it's a nice job," DuQuesne said, admiringly. "I've built complex stuff myself, but he's got me completely lost. It'd take a week to find out where some of the stuff is going and what it's going to do when it gets there."

Straightening up, the slave clamped several electrodes to his head and motioned to Seaton and the others, speaking to Dorothy as he did so.

"He wants to put those things on our heads," she translated, "but I can't make out what they're for. Shall we let him?"

"Yes," he decided instantly. "There's going to be hell to pay any minute now, and no pitch hot. I got us in too deep to back out now. Besides, I've got a hunch. But of course I'm not trying to decide for any of you. In fact, Dot, it might be smart if you . . ."

"I'm not smart, Dick. Where you go, I go," Dorothy said quietly, and bent her auburn head to be fitted.

"I do not relish the idea," Crane said. "In fact, I do not like it at all. But, under present circumstances, it seems the thing to do."

Margaret followed Crane's lead, but DuQuesne said, with a sneer, "Go ahead; let him make zombies of you. Nobody wires me up to a machine I can't understand."

The slave closed a switch, and—instantly—the four visitors acquired a completely detailed knowledge of the languages and customs of both Mardonale, the nation in which they now were, and of Kondal, the nation to which the slaves belonged, the only two civilized nations upon Osnome.

While amazement at this method of instruction was still upon the Earthmen's faces the slave—or, as they now knew him, Dunark, the kofedix or crown prince of Kondal— began to remove the helmets. He took off the girls', and Crane's. He was reaching for Seaton's when there was a flash, a crackle, and a puff of smoke from the machine. Dunark and Seaton both fell flat.

Before Crane could reach them, however, they both recovered and Dunark said, "This is a mechanical educator, something entirely new. We've been working on it several years, but it is still very crude. I didn't like to use it, but I had to, to warn you of what Nalboon is going to do and to convince you that saving your own lives would save ours as well. But something went wrong, probably because of my hasty work in assembly. Instead of stopping at teaching you our languages it shorted me and Dick together—completely."

"What would such a short do?" Crane asked.

"I'll answer that, Dunark." Seaton had not recovered quite as fast as the Kondalian, but was now back to normal.

"All it did was to print in the brain of each of us, down to the finest detail, everything that the other had ever learned. It was the completeness of the transfer that put us both out for a minute."

"I'm sorry, Seaton, believe me. . . ."

"Why?" Seaton grinned. "It's taken each of us all our lives to learn what we know, and now it's doubled. We're both 'way ahead, aren't we?"

"I certainly am, and I'm very glad that you take it that way. But time presses. . . ."

"Let me tell 'em." Seaton said. "You aren't exactly sure which English to use yet, the one I talk or the one I write, and neither you nor we can think very fast, yet, in the other's language. I'll boil it down.

"This is Crown Prince Dunark of Kondal. The other thirteen are relatives of his, princes and princesses. Nalboon's raiders got them while they were out hunting—used a new kind of nerve-gas so they couldn't kill themselves, which is good technique in these parts.

"Kondal and Mardonale have been at war for over six thousand years, a war with no holds barred. No prisoners, except to find out what they know; no niceties. Having found out what these Kondalians knew, Nalboon threw a party—a Roman circus, really—and was going to feed them to some pet devil-fish of his when those armored flying animals—karlono, they call them—smelled them and came into the picture.

"You know what happened then. These people were aboard Nalboon's plane, the one we eased down to the ground. You'd think Nalboon would think he owed us something, but . . ."

"Let me finish," Dunark cut in. "You simply will not do yourself justice. Having saved his life, you should have been guests of the most honored kind. You would have been, anywhere else in the universe. But no Mardonalian has, or ever has had, either honor or conscience. At first, Nalboon was afraid of you, as were we all. We thought you were from the fifteenth sun, now at its closest possible distance, and after seeing your power we expected annihilation.

"However, after seeing the *Skylark* as a machine, learning that you are short of power, and finding you gentle—weak, he thinks that is; how wrong he is!—instead of bloodthirsty, Nalboon decided to kill you and take your ship, with its wonderful new power. For, while we Osnomians are ignorant of chemistry, we know machines and we know electricity. No Osnomian has ever had any inkling that such a thing as atomic energy exists. Nevertheless, after his study of your engines, Nalboon knows how to liberate it and how to control it. With the *Skylark* he could obliterate Kondal; and to do that, he would do anything.

"Also, he or any other Osnomian scientist, including myself, would go to any length, would challenge First Cause itself, to secure even one of those small containers of the chemical you call *salt*. It is the scarcest, most precious substance in our world. You actually had more of it at the table than the total previously known to exist upon all Osnome. Its immense value is due, not to its rarity, but to the fact that it is the only known catalyst for our hardest metals.

"You know now why Nalboon intends to kill you; and nothing you can do or not do will alter that intent. His plan is this: during the next sleeping period—I simply can't use your word 'night,' since there is no such thing on Osnome—he will cut into the *Skylark* and take all the salt you have in it. The interrupted circus will be resumed, with you Tellurians as principal guests. We Kondalians will be given to the karlono. Then you five will be killed and your bodies smelted to recover the salt that is in them.

"This is the warning I had to give you. Its urgency explains why I used my crude educator. In self-defense, I must add this—the lives of you five Tellurians are not of paramount importance, the lives of us fourteen Kondalians much less so. We are all expendable. The *Skylark*, however, is not. If Nalboon gets her, every living Kondalian will die within a year. That fact, and that fact alone, explains why you saw me, the kofedix of Kondal, prostrate myself before Nalboon of Mardonale, and heard me order my kinsmen to do the same."

"How do you, a prince of another nation, know all these things?" Crane asked.

"Some are common knowledge. I heard much while aboard Nalboon's plane. I read Nalboon's plan from the brain of the officer Dick killed. He was a . . . a colonel of the guard, and high in Nalboon's favor. He was to have been in charge of cutting into the *Skylark* and of killing and smelting you five."

"That clears things up," Seaton said. "Thanks, Dunark. The big question now is, what do we do about it?"

"I suggest that you take us into the *Skylark* and get away from here—as soon as you can. I'll pilot you to Kondalek, our capital city. There, I can assure you, you will be welcomed as you deserve. My father will treat you as a visiting karfedix should be treated. As far as I am concerned, if you can succeed in getting us back to Kondal—or in getting the *Skylark* there without any of us—nothing I can ever do will lighten the burden of my indebtedness; but I promise you all the copper you want, and anything else you may desire that is within the power of all Kondal to give."

Seaton scowled in thought.

"Our best chance is with you," he said, finally. "But if we give you atomic power, which we would be doing if we take you back home, Kondal will obliterate Mardonale—if you can."

"Of course."

"So, ethically, perhaps we should leave you all here and try to blast our own way to the *Skylark*. Then go on about our own business."

"That is your right."

"But I couldn't do it. And if I did, Dottie would skin me alive and rub salt in, every day from now on . . . and Nalboon and his crowd are the scum of the universe. . . . Maybe I'm prejudiced by having your whole mind in mine, but I think I'd have to come to the same decision if I had Nalboon's whole mind in there as well. When will we make the break—the hour after the second meal?"

"The strolling hour, yes. You are using my knowledge, I see, just as I am using yours."

"Mart and DuQuesne, we'll make our break just after the next meal, when everybody is strolling around talking to everybody else. That's when the guards are most lax, and our best chance, since we haven't got armor and no good way of getting any."

"But how about your killing his guards and blowing the end out of his palace?" DuQuesne asked. "He isn't the type to take much of that sitting down. Won't that make him hurry things along?"

"We don't quite know, either Dunark or I. It depends pretty much on which emotion is governing, anger or fear. But we'll know pretty quick. He'll be paying us a call of state pretty soon now and we'll see what he acts like and how he talks. However, he's quite a diplomat and may conceal his real feelings entirely. But remember, he thinks gentleness is fear, so don't be surprised if I open up on him. If he gets the least bit tough I'll cut him down to size right then."

"Well," Crane said, "if we have some time to wait, we may as well wait in comfort instead of standing up in the middle of the room. I, for one, would like to ask a few questions."

The Tellurians seated themselves upon divans and Dunark began to dismantle the machine he had built. The Kondalians remained standing behind their "masters," until Seaton protested.

"Please sit down, everybody. There's no need of keeping up this farce of your being slaves as long as we're alone."

"Perhaps not, but at the first sign of a visitor we must all be in our places. Now that we have a little time and are able to understand each other, I will introduce my party to yours.

"Fellow Kondalians, greet Karfedix Seaton and Karfedix Crane, of a strange and extremely distant planet called Earth." He and his group saluted formally. "Greet also the noble ladies, Miss Vaneman and Miss Spencer, soon to become Karfedir Seaton and Karfedir Crane, respectively." They saluted again.

"Guests from Earth, allow me to present the Kofedir Sitar, the only one of my wives who was unfortunate enough to be with me on our ill-fated hunting expedition." One of the women stepped forward and bowed deeply to the four, who returned the compliment in kind.

Ignoring DuQuesne as a captive, he went on to introduce the other Kondalians as his brothers, sisters, half-brothers, half-sisters, and cousins—all members of the ruling house of Kondal.

"Now, after I have had a word with you in private, Doctor Seaton, I will be glad to give the others any information I can."

"I want a word with you, too, Junior. I didn't want to break up your ceremony by arguing about it out there, but I am not, never was, and never will be a karfedix—which word, as you know, translates quite closely into 'emperor.' I'm merely a plain citizen."

"I know that . . . that is, I know it, in a way, from your own knowledge; but I find it impossible to understand it or to relate it to anything in my own experience. Nor can I understand your government; I fail entirely to see how it could function for even one of your years without breaking down. On Osnome, Dick, men of your attainments, and Martin's, are karfedo. You will be, whether you want to or not. Ph.D. . . . Doctor of Philosophy . . . Karfedix of Knowledge . . ."

"Pipe down, Dunark—forget it! What was it you wanted to talk to me about away from the mob?"

"Dorothy and Margaret. You already have it in your mind somewhere, from mine, but you might find it as impossible to understand as I do much of yours. Your women are so different from ours, so startlingly beautiful, that Nalboon will not kill either of them—for a time. So, if worst comes to worst, be sure to kill them both while you still can."

"I see . . . yes, I find it now." Seaton's voice was cold, his eyes hard. "Thanks. I'll remember that, and charge it to Nalboon's personal account."

Rejoining the others, they found Dorothy and Sitar deep in conversation.

"So a man has half a dozen or so wives?" Dorothy was asking in surprise. "How can you get along—I'd fight like a wildcat if Dick got any such funny ideas as that!"

"Why, splendidly, of course. I wouldn't *think* of ever marrying a man if he was such a . . . a . . . a *louse* that only one woman would have him!"

"I've got a cheerful thought for you and Peg, Red-top. Dunark here thinks you two are beautiful. 'Startlingly beautiful' was the exact description."

"What? In this light? Green, black, yellow, and mudcolor? We're positively hideous! And if that's your idea of a joke . . ."

"Oh, no, Dorthee," Sitar interposed. "You two are beautiful—really lovely. And you have such a rich, smoothly-blending color-flow. It's a shame to hide so much of it with robes."

"Yes, why do you? Dunark asked; as both girls blushed hotly, he paused, obviously searching in Dick's mind for an answer he could not find in his own. "I mean, I see the sense of covering as a protection, or for certain ceremonials in which covering is ritual; but when not needed, in fact, when you are too warm, as you are now . . ." He broke off in embarrassment and went on, "Help, Dick. I seem to be getting my foot in it deeper and deeper. What have I done to offend?"

"Nothing. It isn't you at all; it's just that our race has worn clothing for centuries, and can't . . . Mart, how would you explain 'modesty' to race like that?" He swept his arm to cover the group of perfectly poised, completely un-self-conscious, naked men and women.

"I could explain it, after a fashion, but I doubt very much if even you, Dunark, with your heredity, could understand it. Sometime, when we have a few hours to spare, I will try to, if you like. But in the meantime, what are those collars and what do they mean?"

"Identifications. When a child is nearly grown, it is cast about his neck. It bears his name, national number, and the device of his house. Being made of arenak, it cannot be altered without killing the person. Any Osnomian not wearing a collar is unthinkable; but if it should ever happen he would be killed."

"Is that belt something similar? No, it . . ."

"No. Merely a pouch. But even Nalboon thought it was opaque arenak, so didn't try to open it."

"Is that transparent armor made of the same thing?"

"Yes, except that nothing is added to the matrix to make it colored or opaque. It is in the preparation of this metal that salt is indispensable. It acts only as a catalyst, being recovered afterward, but neither nation has ever had enough salt to make all the armor they want."

"Aren't those monsters—karlono, I think you called them—covered with the same thing? And what are they, anyway?" Dorothy asked.

"Yes. It is thought that the beasts grow it, just as fishes grow scales. But no one knows how they do it—or even how they can possibly do it. Very little is known about them, however, except that they are the worst scourge of Osnome. Various scientists have described the karlon as a bird, a beast, a fish, and a vegetable; sexual, asexual, and hermaphroditic. Its habitat is—"

The gong sounded and the Kondalians leaped to their positions. The kofedix went to the door. Nalboon brushed him aside and entered, escorted by a squad of heavily-armed, full-armored soldiers. A scowl of anger was on his face; he was plainly in an ugly mood.

"Stop, Nalboon of Mardonale!" Seaton thundered, in the Mardonalian tongue and at the top of his powerful voice. "Dare you invade privacy without invitation?"

The escort shrank back, but the emperor stood his ground, although he was plainly taken by surprise. With a heroic effort he smoothed his face into lines of cordiality.

"May I inquire why my guards are slain and my palace destroyed by my honored guest?"

"You may. I permit it, to point out your errors. Your guards, at your order, no doubt, sought to invade my privacy. Being forbearing, I warned them once, but one of them was foolhardy enough to challenge me, and was of course destroyed. Then the others attempted to raise their childish weapons against me, and I of course destroyed them. The wall merely chanced to be inside the field of action of the force I chanced to be employing at the time.

"An honored guest? Bah! Know, Nalboon, that when you seek to treat as captive a visiting domak of my race, you lose not only your own life, but the lives of all your nation as well. Do you perceive your errors?"

Anger and fear fought for supremacy on Nalboon's face; but a third emotion, wonder, won. He, Nalboon, was armed: he had with him a score of armed and armored men. This stranger had nothing; the slaves were less than nothing. Yet he stood there, arrogantly confident, master of the planet, the solar system, and the universe, by his bearing . . . and how . . . *how* had he completely obliterated fifty armed and armored men and a thousand tons of stone and ultra-hard metal? Nalboon temporized.

"May I ask how you, so recently ignorant, know our language?"

"You may not. You may go."

chapter **18**

"THAT WAS A BEAUTIFUL BLUFF, DICK!" Dunark exclaimed, as the door closed behind Nalboon and his guards. "Exactly the right tone—you've got him guessing plenty."

"It got him, all right—for the moment—but I'm wondering how long it will hold him. He's a big time operator, and smart. The smart thing for us to do, I think, would be to take off for the *Skylark* right now, before he can get organized. What do you think, Mart?"

"I think so. We're altogether too vulnerable here."

The Earth-people quickly secured the few personal things they had brought with them. Seaton stepped out into the hall, waved the guards away, and motioned Dunark to lead the way. The other Kondalians fell in behind, as usual, and the group walked boldly toward the exit nearest the landing dock. The guards offered no opposition, but stood at attention and saluted as they passed. The officer lifted his microphone, however, and Seaton knew that Nalboon was being kept informed of every development.

Outside the palace, Dunark turned his head.

"Run!" he snapped. All did so. "If they get a flyer into the air before we reach the dock it'll be just too bad. There'll be no pursuit from the palace—it isn't expendable—but the dock will be tough."

Rounding a metal statue some fifty feet from the base of the towering dock they saw that the door of one of the elevators was open and that two guards stood just inside it. At sight of the party the guards raised their guns; but, fast as they were, Seaton was faster. At first sight of the open door he had taken two quick steps and hurled himself across the intervening forty feet in a football plunge. Before the two soldiers could bring their guns to bear he crashed into them, hurling them across the cage and crushing them against its metal wall.

"Good work," Dunark said. He stripped the unconscious guards of their weapons and, after asking Seaton's permission, distributed them among the men of his party. "Now, perhaps, we can surprise whoever is on the roof. That was why you didn't shoot?"

"No," Seaton grunted. "We need this elevator. It wouldn't be much good after taking even a Mark One load." He threw the two Mardonalians out of the elevator and closed the door.

Dunark took the controls. The elevator shot upward, stopping at a level well below the top. He took a tubular device from his belt and fitted it over the muzzle of the Mardonalian pistol.

"We get out here," Dunark said, "and go up the rest of the way by side stairs that aren't used much. We'll meet a few guards, probably, but I can take care of them. Stay behind me, please, everybody."

Seaton promptly objected and Dunark went on, "No, Dick, stay back. You know as much about this as I do, I know, but you can't get at the knowledge as fast. I'll let you take over when we reach the top."

Dunark took the lead, his pistol resting lightly against his hip. At the first turn of the corridor they came upon four guards. The pistol did not leave Dunark's hip, but were four subdued clicks, in faster succession than a man could count, and four men dropped.

"What a silencer!" DuQuesne whispered to Seaton. "I didn't suppose a silencer could work that fast."

"They don't use powder," Seaton replied absently, all his faculties pinned to the next corner. "Force-field projection."

Dunark disposed of several more groups of guards before the head of the last stairway was reached. He stopped there.

"Now, Dick, you take over. I'm speaking English so I won't have to order each of my men individually—command them, literally—not to take my place at your side. We'll need all the speed and all the fire-power you have. There are hundreds of men on the roof outside, with rapid-fire cannon throwing a thousand shells a minute. If Crane will give me his pistols you can kick that door open as soon as you're ready."

"I've got a lot better idea than that," DuQuesne said. "I'm as fast as you are, Seaton, and, like you, I can use both hands. Give me the guns and we'll have 'em cleaned out before the door gets fully open."

"That's a thought, brother—that's *really* a thought." Seaton said. "Hand 'em over, Mart. Ready, Blackie? On your mark—get set—go!"

He kicked the door open and there was a stuttering crash as the four weapons burst into almost continuous flame—a crash obliterated by an overwhelming concatenation of sound as the X-plosive bullets, sweeping the roof with a rapidly-opening fan of death, struck their marks and exploded.

It was well that the two men in the doorway were past masters in the art of handling their weapons—and that they had in their bullets the force of giant shells! For rank upon rank of soldiery were massed there; engines of destruction covered elevators, doorways, and approaches.

So fast and fierce was the attack that trained gunners had no time to press their switches. The battle lasted approximately one second. It was over while shattered remnants of the guns and fragments of the metal and stone of the dock were still falling, through a fine mist of what had once been men.

Assured that not a single Mardonalian remained upon the dock, Seaton waved emphatically to the others.

"Snap it up!" he yelled. "This going to be hotter than the middle tail-race of Hades in exactly one minute."

He led the way across the dock toward the *Skylark*, choosing the path with care between yawning holes. The ship was still in place, still held immovable by the attractor, but what a sight she was! Her quartz windows were shattered, her Norwegian-armor skin was dented and warped and fissured, half her plating was gone.

Not a shot had struck her. All this damage had been done by flying fragments of the guns and of the dock itself; and Seaton and Crane, who had developed the new explosive, were aghast at its awful power.

They climbed hastily into the vessel and Seaton ran toward the controls.

"I hear battleships," Dunark said. "Is it permitted that I operate one of your machine guns?"

"Go as far as you like!"

While Seaton was reaching for the speed-lever the first ranging shell from the first warship exploded against the side of the dock, just below them. His hand grasped the lever just as the second shell screamed through the air, scant yards above them; and as he shot the *Skylark* into the air under five notches of power a stream of the huge projectiles poured through the spot where she had just been.

Crane and DuQuesne aimed several shots at the battleships, but the range was so extreme that no damage was done. Dunark's rifle, however, was making a continuous chatter and they turned toward him. He was shooting, not at the warships, but at the city growing so rapidly smaller beneath them. He was moving the gun's muzzle in a small spiral, spraying the entire city with death and destruction. As they looked, the first of the shells reached the ground, just as Dunark ceased firing for back of ammunition. The palace disappeared, blotted out in a cloud of dust; a cloud which spiraled outward until it obscured the area where the city had been.

High enough to be safe, Seaton stopped climbing and went out to confer with the others.

"It sure feels good to get a cool breath," he said, inhaling deeply the thin, cold air of that altitude. Then he saw the Kondalians, who, besides having taken a beating from the—to them—atrocious acceleration, were gasping for breath and were shivering, pale with cold.

"If *this* is what you like," Dunark said, trying manfully to grin, "I see at last why you wear clothes."

Apologizing quickly, Seaton went back to the board and laid a course, on a downward slant, toward the ocean. Then he asked DuQuesne to take over and rejoined the group.

"There's no accounting for tastes," he said to Dunark, "but I can't hand your climate a thing. It's hotter and muggier than Washington in August; 'and that,' as the poet feelingly remarked, 'is going some.' But there's no sense to sitting here in the dark. Snap the switch, will you, Dottie?"

"Be glad to . . . now we'll see what they *really* look like. . . . Why, they *are* beautiful . . . in spite of being sort of greenish like, they *really* are!"

But Sitar took one look at the woman by her side, shut both eyes, and screamed. "What a *horrible* light! Shut it off; *please!* I'd rather be in darkness all my . . ."

"Did you ever see any darkness?" Seaton interrupted.

"Yes, I shut myself into a dark closet once, when I was a girl . . . and it scared me half out of my senses. I'll take back what I started to say; but that light"—Dorothy had already turned it off—"was the most *terrible* thing I ever saw!"

"Why, Sitar," Dorothy said, "You looked perfectly stunning!"

"They see things differently from the way we do," Seaton explained. "Their optic nerves respond differently, send a different message to the brain. The same stimulus produces two entirely different end sensations. Am I making myself clear?"

"Sort of. Not very." Dorothy said, doubtfully.

"Take a concrete example, the Kondalian color 'mlap.' Can you describe it?"

"It's a kind of greenish orange . . . but it shouldn't be. By what we learned from Dunark, it's brilliant purple."

"That's what I mean. Well, get set, everybody, and we'll tear off a few knots for Kondalek."

As they neared the ocean several Mardonalian battleships tried to intercept them; but the *Skylark* hopped over them and her speed was such that pursuit was not attempted. The ocean was crossed at the same high speed.

Dunark, who had already tuned the *Skylark*'s powerful transmitter to his father's private frequency, reported to him everything that had happened; and emperor and crown prince worked out a modified version which was to be broadcast throughout the nation.

Crane drew Seaton aside.

"Do you think we can really trust these Kondalians, any more than we should have trusted the Mardonalians? It might be better for us to stay in the *Skylark* instead of going to the palace at all."

"Yes to the first; no to the second," Seaton replied. "I went off half-cocked last time, I admit; but I've got his whole mind inside my skull, so I know him a lot better than I know you. They've got some mighty funny ideas, and they're bloodthirsty and hard as tungsten carbide; but, basically, they're just as decent as we are.

"As for staying in here, what good would that do? Steel is as soft as mush to the stuff they've got. And we can't go anywhere, anyway. No copper—we're down to the plating in spots. And we couldn't if we were full of copper. The old bus is a wreck; she's got to be completely rebuilt. But you don't have to worry this time, Mart. I know they're friends of ours."

"You don't say that very often," Crane conceded, "and when you do, I believe you. All objections are withdrawn."

Flying over an immense city, the *Skylark* came to a halt directly above the palace, which, with its landing dock near by, was very similar to that of Nalboon, the Mardonalian potentate.

From the city beneath the *Skylark* hundreds of big guns roared in welcome. Banners and streamers hung from every point. The air became tinted and perfumed with a bewildering variety of colors and scents. Ether and air alike were full of messages of welcome and hymns of joy.

A fleet of giant warships came up, to escort the battered little globe with impressive ceremony down to the landing dock; while around them great numbers of smaller aircraft flitted. Tiny one-man machines darted here and there, apparently always in imminent danger of collision with each other or with their larger fellows, but always escaping as though by a miracle. Beautiful pleasure-planes soared and dipped and wheeled like great gulls; and, cleaving their stately way through the hordes of lesser craft, immense multi-plane passenger liners partially supported by helicopter screws turned aside from their scheduled courses to pay homage to the half of the Kondalian royal family so miraculously returned from the dead.

As the *Skylark* approached the roof of the dock, all the escorting vessels dropped away. On the roof, instead of the brilliant assemblage the Earthmen had expected to see, there was only a small group of persons, all of whom were as completely unadorned as were Dunark and the other erstwhile captives.

In answer to Seaton's look of surprise, Dunark said, with feeling, "My father, mother, and the rest of the family. They knew we'd be stripped; they are meeting us that way."

Seaton landed the ship. He and his four stayed inside while the family reunion, which was very similar to an Earthly one under similar circumstances, took place. Dunark then led his father up to the *Skylark* and the Tellurians disembarked.

"Friends, I have told you of my father; I present you to Roban, the Karfedix of Kondal. Father, it is an honor to present to you those who rescued us from Nalboon and from Mardonale. Seaton, Karfedix of Knowledge; Crane, Karfedix of Wealth; Miss Vaneman, and Miss Spencer. The Karfedelix DuQuesne"—waving his hand at him—"is a lesser authority of knowledge and is captive to the others."

The Kofedix Dunark exaggerates our services," Seaton said,

"and does not mention the fact that he saved all our lives."

Disregarding Seaton's remark, Roban thanked them in the name of Kondal and introduced them to the rest of his party. As they all walked toward the elevator the emperor turned to his son with a puzzled expression.

"I know that our guests are from a very distant world, and I understand your accident with the educator, but I cannot understand the titles of these men. Knowledge and wealth are not—cannot be—ruled over. Are you sure that you have translated their titles correctly?"

"No translation is possible. Crane has no title, and was not at all willing for me to apply any title to him. Seaton's title, one of learnedness, has no equivalent in our language. What I did was to call them what each one would certainly become if he had been born one of us. Their government is not a government at all, but stark madness, the rulers being chosen by the people themselves, who change their minds and their rulers every year or two. And, everyone being equal before the law, does just about as he pleases. . . ."

"Incredible!" exclaimed Roban. "How, then, is anything done?"

"I do not know. I simply do not understand it at all. They do not seem to care, as a nation, whether anything worth while gets done or not, as long as each man has what he calls his liberty. But that isn't the worst, or the most unreasonable. Listen to this."

Dunark told his father all about the Seaton-Crane versus DuQuesne conflict. "Then, in spite of all that, Crane gave DuQuesne both his pistols and DuQuesne stood at Seaton's side in that doorway and the two of them killed every Mardonalian on that roof before I could fire a single shot. DuQuesne fired every bullet in both his pistols and made no attempt whatever to kill either Seaton or Crane. And he is *still* their captive!"

"Incredible! What an incomprehensibly distorted sense of honor! If it were anyone except you saying this, I would deem it the ravings of a maniac. Are you sure, son, that these are facts?"

"I am sure. I saw them happen; so did the others. But in many other respects they are . . . well, they are not insane . . . incomprehensible. The tenets of reason as we know reason simply are not applicable to many of their ideas, concepts, and actions. Clothing, for instance. Their values, their ethics, are in some respects absolutely incommensurate with ours. However, their sense of honor is, at bottom, as sound as ours,

and as strong. And, since Nalboon tried to kill them, they
are definitely on our side."

"That, at least, I can understand, and it is well." The older
man shook his head. "My mind is full of cobwebs. An enemy
who is a friend. Or vice versa. Or both. A master who arms
a slave. An armed slave who does not kill his master. That,
my son, is simple, plain, stark lunacy!"

During this conversation they had reached the palace, after
traversing grounds even more sumptuous and splendid than
those surrounding the palace of Nalboon. Inside the building,
Dunark himself led the guests to their rooms, accompanied
by the major-domo and an escort of guards. The rooms were
intercommunicating and each had a completely equipped
bathroom, with a small swimming pool, built of polished
metal, in lieu of a tub.

"This'd be nice," Seaton said, indicating the pool, "if you
had some cold water."

"There is cold water." Dunark turned on a ten-inch stream
of lukewarm water, then shut it off and smiled sheepishly.
"But I keep forgetting what you mean by the word 'cold.' We
will install refrigerating machines at once."

"Oh, don't bother about that; we won't be here long
enough. One thing, though, I forgot to tell you. We'll eat
our own food, not yours."

"Of course. We'll take care of it. I'll be back in half an
hour to take you to fourth-meal."

Scarcely had the Earthlings freshened themselves than he
was back; but he was no longer the Dunark they had known.
He now wore a metal-and-leather harness that was one blaze
of gems. A belt hung with resplendent weapons replaced the
familiar hollow one of metal. His right arm, between the wrist
and the elbow, was almost covered by six bracelets of a transparent, deep cobalt-blue metal; each set with an incredibly
brilliant stone of the same color. On his left wrist he wore
a Kondalian chronometer. This was an instrument resembling
an odometer, whose numerous revolving segments showed a
large and constantly-increasing number—the date and time
of the Osnomian day expressed in a decimal number of the
years of Kondalian history.

"Greetings, oh guests from Tellus! I feel more like myself,
now that I am again in my trappings and have my weapons
at my side." He attached a timepiece to the wrist of each of
the guests, with a bracelet of the blue metal. "Will you ac-
company me to fourth-meal or aren't you hungry?"

"We accept with thanks," Dorothy replied, promptly. "I, for one, am starving by inches."

As they walked toward the dining-hall Dunark noticed that Dorothy's eyes kept straying to his bracelets.

"They are our wedding rings. Man and wife exchange bracelets as part of the ceremony."

"Then you can always tell whether a man is married, and how many wives he has, just by looking at his arm. Nice. Some men on Earth wear wedding rings, but not many."

Roban met them at the door of the hall, and Dorothy counted ten of the peculiar bracelets upon his right arm as he led them to places near his own. The room was a replica of the other Osnomian dining-hall they had seen; and the women were decorated with the same barbaric splendor of scintillating gems.

After the meal, which was a happy one, taking on the nature of a celebration in honor of the return of the children, Du-Quesne went directly to his room, while the others spent the time until zero hour in strolling about the grounds. Upon returning to the room occupied by the two girls, the couples separated, each girl accompanying her lover to the door of his room.

Margaret was ill at ease.

"What's the matter, sweetheart?" Crane asked, solicitously.

She twisted nervously at a button on his shirt.

"I didn't know that you . . . I wasn't . . . I mean I didn't . . ." She broke off, then went on with a rush. "What did Dunark mean by calling you the Karfedix of Wealth?"

"Well, you see, I happen to have some money . . ." he began.

"Then you really are M. Reynolds Crane!"

Crane put his other arm around her, kissed her, and held her close.

"Is *that* all that was bothering you? What does money amount to between you and me?"

"Nothing—to me—but I'm awfully glad I didn't know anything about it before." She returned his kisses with fervor. "That is, it doesn't mean a thing if you are *perfectly* sure that I'm not after—"

Crane, the imperturbable, broke a hard and fast rule and interrupted her. "Don't say that, dear. Don't even think of it, ever again. We both know that between you and me there never have been, are not now, and never shall be, any doubts or any questions."

"If I could have that tank full of good cold water right now," Seaton said, as he stood with Dorothy in the door of his room, "I'd throw you in, clothes and all, dive in with you, and we'd soak in it all night. Night? What do I mean, night? This constant daylight, constant heat, and supersaturated humidity are pulling my cork. You don't look up to snuff, either." He lifted her gorgeous auburn head from his shoulder and studied her face. "You look like you'd been pulled through a knothole—you're starting to get black circles under your eyes."

"I know it." She nestled even closer against him. "I'm scared blue half the time. I always thought I had good nerves, but every thing here is so perfectly *horrible* that I can't sleep—and I always used to go to sleep in the air, two or three inches before I hit the sheets. When I'm with you it isn't too bad—I really enjoy a lot of the things—but the sleeping-periods—Ugh!" She shivered in the circle of his arms. "You can say anything about them you can think of, and I'll back you to your proverbial nineteen decimals. I just lie there, tenser and tighter, and my mind goes up like a skyrocket. Peggy and I just huddle up to each other in a ghastly purple funk. I'm ashamed of both of us, but that's the way it is and we can't help it."

"I'm sorry, ace." He tightened his arms. "Sorrier than I can say. You've got nerve, and you aren't going to fall apart; I know that. It's just that you haven't roughed it away from home enough to be able to feel at home wherever your hat is. The reason you feel safe with me is probably that I feel perfectly at home here myself—except for the temperature and so on."

"Uh-huh . . . probably." Dorothy gnawed at her lower lip. "I never thought I was a clinging-vine type, but I'm getting to be. I'm simply scared to death to go to bed."

"Chin up, sweetheart." An interlude. "I wish I could be with you all the time—you know how much I wish it—but it won't be long. We'll fix the chariot and snap back to Earth in a hurry."

She pushed him into his room, followed him inside, closed the door, and put both hands on his shoulders.

"Dick Seaton," she said, blushing hotly, "You're not as dumb as I thought you were—you're dumber! But if you won't say it, even after such a sob-story as that, I will. No law says that a marriage *has* to be performed on Earth to be legal."

He pressed her close; his emotion so great that for a minute he could not talk. Then he said, "I never thought of anything like that, Dottiegirl." His voice was low and vibrant. "If I had, I wouldn't have dared say it out loud. With you so far away from home, it'd seem . . ."

"It wouldn't seem anything of the kind," she denied, without waiting to find out what it was that she was denying. Don't you see, you big, thick-headed, wonderful lug, it's the only thing to do? We need each other—at least I need you so much . . ."

"Say 'each other'—it's right," he declared fervently.

"The family would like to have seen me married, of course . . . but there are some advantages, even there. Dad would hate a grand Washington wedding, and so would you. It's better all around to be married here."

Seaton, who had been trying to get a word in, silenced her.

"I'm convinced, Dottie, have been ever since I came out of shock. I'm so glad I can't express it. I've been scared stiff every time I've thought about our wedding. I'll speak to the karfedix the first thing in the morning . . . or say, how'd it be to wake him up and have it done right now?"

"Oh, Dick, be reasonable!" Dorothy's eyes, however, danced with glee. "That would never do. Tomorrow will be too awfully sudden, as it is. And Dick, please speak to Martin, will you? Peggy's scared a lot worse than I am, and Martin, the dear old stupid jerk, is a lot less likely than even you are to think of being prime mover in anything like this. And Peggy's afraid to suggest it to him. Said she'd curl right up and die; and she just about would."

"Ah. Aha!" Seaton straightened up and held her out at arms' length. "A light dawns. I thought there was something fishy about your walking me home. Queer—like a nine-dollar bill. It didn't register, even at 'sob-story'—I thought my bad example was corrupting your English. A put-up job, eh?"

"What do you think? That I'd have the nerve to do it all by myself? But not all, Dick." She snuggled up to him again, blissfully content. "Just the littlest, teeniest bit of it, was all."

Seaton opened the door. "Mart, bring Peggy over here!"

"Heavens, Dick! Be careful! You'll spoil everything!"

"No, I won't. Leave it to me—I bashfully admit that I'm a blinding flash and a deafening report at this diplomacy stuff. Smooth, like an eel." The other two joined them.

"Dottie and I have been talking things over, and have decided that today would be the best possible day for a wedding. She's afraid of these long daylight nights, and I'd sleep a lot better if I knew where she was all the time instead of part of it. She's willing, if you two see it the same way and

make it a double. So how about it? And if you say anything
but 'yes' I'll tie you, Mart, up like a pretzel; and take you,
Peg, over my knee and spank you. I'll give you one whole
second to think it over."

Margaret blushed furiously but pressed herself closer against
Crane's side.

"That's time enough for me," Crane said. "A marriage
here would be recognized anywhere, I think . . . with the
certificate registered . . . if the final court declared it invalid
we could be married again. . . . Considering all the circumstances, it would be the best thing for everyone concerned."
Crane's lean, handsome face assumed a darker color as he
looked down at Margaret's sparkling eyes and happily animated
face. "Nothing else in existence is as certain as our love. It
is of course the bride's privilege to set the date. Peggy?"

"The sooner the better," Margaret said, blushing again.
"Did you say today, Dick?"

"That's what I said. I'll see the karfedix about it as soon
as we get up," and the two couples separated.

"I'm just too perfectly happy for words," Dorothy whispered into Seaton's ear as he kissed her goodnight. "I simply
don't care whether I sleep a wink tonight or not."

chapter **19**

SEATON WOKE UP, HOT AND UNCOMFORT-
able, but with a great surge of joy in his heart—this was his
wedding day! Springing out of bed, he released the full stream
of "cold" water, filling the pool in a few moments. Poising
lightly on the edge, he made a clean, sharp dive—and yelled
in surprise as he came snorting to the surface. For Dunark
had made his promise good; the water was only a couple
of degrees above the freezing point! After a few minutes of
swimming and splashing in the icy water he rubbed himself
down, shaved, put on shirt and slacks, and lifted his powerful
bass voice in the wedding chorus from "The Rose Maiden."

"Rise, sweet maid, arise, arise;
"Rise, sweet maid, arise, arise;
" 'Tis the last fair morning for thy maiden eyes,"

he sang lustily, out of his sheer joy in being alive, and was surprised to hear three other voices—soprano, contralto, and tenor—continue the song from the adjoining room. He opened the door.

"Good morning, Dick, you sounded happy," Crane said.

"So did you all, but who wouldn't be? Look what today is!" He embraced Dorothy ardently. "Besides, I found some cold water this morning."

"Everybody within a mile heard you discover it," Dorothy giggled. "We warmed ours up a little. I like a cold bath, too, but not in ice-water. B-r-r-r!"

"But I didn't know you two boys could sing." Margaret said.

"We can't," Seaton assured her. "We just barber-shop it now and then, for fun. But it sounded as though you can really *sing*."

"I'll say she can sing!" Dorothy exclaimed. "I didn't know it 'til just now, but she's soprano soloist in the First Episcopal, no less!"

"Whee!" Seaton whistled." "If she can stand the strain, we'll have to give this quartet a workout some day—when there's nobody around."

All four became silent, thinking of the coming event of the day, until Crane said, "They have ministers here, I know, and I know something of their religion, but my knowledge is vague. You know more about it than we do, Dick—tell us about it while we wait."

Seaton paused a moment, and odd look on his face. As one turning the pages of an unfamiliar book of reference, he was seeking the answer to Crane's question in the vast store of Osnomian information received from Dunark. He spoke slower than usual, and used much better English, when he replied.

"As well as I can explain it, it's a very peculiar mixture, partly theology, partly Darwinian evolution or its Osnomian equivalent, and partly pure pragmatism or economic determinism. They believe in a supreme being, the First Cause being its nearest English equivalent. They recognize the existence of an immortal and unknowable life-principle, or soul. They believe that the First Cause has laid down the survival of the fittest as the fundamental law, which belief accounts for their perfect physiques. . . ."

"Perfect physiques! Why, they're as weak as children!" Dorothy exclaimed.

"That's because of the low gravity," Seaton explained. "You see, a man of my size weighs only about eighty-six pounds here, on a spring balance, so he wouldn't need any more muscle than a boy of twelve or so on Earth. Either one of you girls could easily handle any two of the strongest men on Osnome. It'd probably take all the strength Dunark has, just to stand up on Earth.

"Considering that fact, they are magnificently developed. They have attained this state by centuries of weeding out the unfit. They have no hospitals for the feeble-minded or the feeble-bodied; all such are executed. The same reasoning accounts for their cleanliness, physical and moral—vice is practically unknown. Clean thinking and clean living are rewarded by the production of a better mental and physical type. . . ."

"Especially since they correct wrong living by those terrible punishments Dunark told us about," Margaret put in.

"Perhaps, although the point is debatable. They also believe that the higher the type, the faster the evolution and the sooner will mankind reach what they call the Ultimate Goal and know all things. Believing as they do that the fittest must survive, and of course thinking themselves the superior type, it is ordained that Mardonale must be destroyed utterly, root and branch.

"Their ministers are chosen from the very fittest, next to the royal family, which is, and must remain, tops. If it doesn't, it ceases to be the royal family and a fitter family takes over. Anyway, ministers are strong, vigorous, and clean, and are almost always high army officers as well as ministers."

An attendant announced the coming of the emperor and his son, to pay the call of state; and, after the ceremonious greetings had been exchanged, all went into the dining-hall for first-meal. After eating, Seaton brought up the question of the double wedding. The emperor was overjoyed.

"Karfedix Seaton, nothing could please us more than to have such a ceremony performed in our palace. Marriage between such highly-evolved persons as are you four is demanded by the First Cause, whose servants we all are. Aside from that, it is an unheard-of honor for any ruler to have even one other karfedix married under his roof, and you are granting me the honor of two! I thank you, and assure you that we will do our best to make the occasion memorable."

"Nothing fancy, please," Seaton said. "Just a simple, plain wedding will do very nicely."

"I will summon Karbix Tarnan to perform the ceremony," Roban said, paying no attention to Seaton's remark. "Our customary time for ceremonies is just before fourth-meal. Is that time satisfactory to all concerned?"

It was entirely satisfactory.

"Dunark, since you are more familiar than I with the customs of our illustrious visitors, you will take charge." Emperor Roban strode out of the room.

Dunark took up his microphone and sent out call after call after call.

Dorothy's eyes sparkled. "They must be going to make a production out of our weddings, Dick—the Karbix is the highest dignitary of the church, isn't he?"

"Yes, as well as being commander-in-chief of all the armed forces of Kondal. Next to Roban he's the most powerful man in the whole empire. They're going to throw a brawl, all right—it'll make the biggest Washington wedding you ever saw look like some small fry's birthday party. And how you'll hate it!"

"Uh-huh, I do already." She laughed rapturously. "I'll cry bitter and salty tears all over the place—I don't think. It's you that will suffer—in silence, I hope?"

"As silently as possible—check." He grinned; and she became, all of a sudden, serious.

"I've always wanted a big wedding, Dick—but remember I wanted to give it up and thought I had."

"I'll remember that always, sweetheart. As I have said before and am about to say again, you're a blinding flash and a deafening report—the universe's best."

As Dunark finished his telephoning, Seaton spoke to him.

"Dottie said, a while back, she'd like to have a few yards of that tapestry-fabric for a dress . . . but, say, she's going to get one anyway, only finer and fancier."

"Just so," Dunark agreed. "In high state ceremonials we always wear robes of state. But you two men, for some reason or other, do not wish to wear them."

"We'll wear white slacks and sport shirts. As you know—if you can find the knowledge—while the women of our race go in for ornamental dress, most of the men do not."

"True." Dunark frowned in perplexity. "Another one of those incomprehensible oddities. However, since your dress will be something no Kondalian has ever seen, it will actually be more resplendant than the robes of your brides.

"I have called in our most expert weavers and tailors, to make the gowns. Before they arrive, let us discuss the ceremony and decide what it will be. You are all somewhat familiar with our customs, but on this I make very sure. Each couple is married twice. The first marriage is symbolized by the exchange of plain bracelets. This marriage lasts two years, during which period either may divorce the other by announcing the fact."

"Hmmm . . ." Crane said. "Some such system of trial marriage is advocated among us every few years, but they all so
surely degenerate into free love that none has found a foothold."

"We have no such trouble. You see, before the first marriage each couple, from lowest to highest, is given a mental
examination. Any person whose graphs show moral turpitude
is shot."

No questions being asked, Dunark went on, "At the end
of the two years the second marriage, which is indissoluble,
is performed. Jeweled bracelets are substituted for the plain
ones. In the case of highly-evolved persons, it is permitted that
the two ceremonies be combined into one. Then there is a
third cremony, used only in the marriage of persons of the
very highest evolution, in which eternal vows are taken and
the faidon, the eternal jewel, is exchanged. I am virtually certain that all four of you are in the eternal class, but that isn't
enough. I must be absolutely certain. Hence, if either couple
elects the eternal ceremony, I must examine that couple here
and now. Otherwise, and should one of you be rejected by
Tarnan, not only would my head roll, but my father would
be intolerably disgraced."

"Huh? Why?" Seaton demanded.

"Because I am responsible," Dunark replied, quietly. "You
heard my father give me the responsibility of seeing to it that
your marriages, the first of their kind in Kondalian history,
are carried out as they should be. If such a frightful thing as
a rejection occurred it would be my fault. I would be decapitated, there and then, as an incompetent. My father would kill
himself, because only an incompetent would delegate an important undertaking to an incompetent."

"What a code!" Seaton whispered to Crane, under his
breath. "What a code!" Then, to Dunark, "But suppose you
pass me and Tarnan doesn't? Then what?"

"That cannot possibly happen. Mind graphs do not lie and
cannot possibly be falsified. However, there is no coercion. You
are at perfect liberty to elect any one of the three marriages
you choose. What is your choice?"

"I want to be married for good, the longer the better. I
vote for the eternal, Dunark. Bring out your test-kit."

"So do I, Dunark," Dorothy said, catching her breath.

"One question first," Crane said. "Would that mean that

my wife would be breaking her vows if she married again
after my death?"

"By no means. Young men are being killed every day; their
wives are expected to marry again. Most men have more than
one wife. Any number of men and women may be linked that
way after death—just as in your chemistry varying numbers
of atoms unite to form stable compounds."

Crane and Margaret agreed that they, too, wanted to be
married forever.

"In your case rings will be substituted for bracelets. After
the ceremony you men may discard them if you like."

"Not me!" Seaton declared. "I'll wear them all the rest of
my life," and Crane expressed the same thought.

"The preliminary examination, then. Put on these helmets,
please." He handed one each to Dorothy and Seaton, and
donned one himself. He pressed a button, and instantly the
two could read each other's mind to the minutest detail; and
each knew that Dunark was reading the minds of both. More-
over, he was studying minutely a device he held in both hands.

"You two pass. I knew you would," he said, and, a couple
of minutes later, he said the same thing to Crane and Margaret.

"I was sure," Dunark said, "but in this case knowing it
wasn't enough. I had to prove it, incontrovertibly. But the
robe-makers have been waiting. You two girls will go with
them, please."

As the girls left Dunark said, "While I was in Mardonale
I heard scraps of talk about a military discovery, besides the
gas whose effects we felt. I heard also that both secrets had
been stolen from Kondal. There was some gloating, in fact,
that we were to be destroyed by our own inventions. I have
learned here that what I heard was true."

"Well, that's easily fixed," Seaton said. "Let's get the
Skylark fixed up and we'll hop over there and jerk Nalboon
out of his palace—if there is any palace and if he's still alive
—and read his mind. If not Nalboon, somebody else. Check?"

"It's worth trying, anyway," Dunark said. "In any event
we must repair the Skylark and replenish her supply of copper
as soon as possible."

The three men went out to the wrecked spaceship and went
through it with care. Inside damage was extensive and serious;
many instruments were broken, including one of the object-
compasses focused upon Earth.

"It's a good thing you had three of 'em, Mart. I've got to

hand it to you for using the old think-tank," Seaton said, as he tossed the useless equipment out upon the dock.

"Better save them, Dick," Dunark said. "You may have use for them later."

"Uh-uh. All they're good for is scrap."

"Then I'll save them. I may need that kind of scrap, some day." He issued orders that all discarded instruments and apparatus were to be stored.

"Well, I suppose the first thing to do is to set up some hydraulic jacks and start straightening," Seaton said.

"Why not throw away this soft stuff and build it of arenak?" Dunark suggested. "You have plenty of salt."

"That's really a thought. Yes, two years' supply. Around a hundred pounds, at a guess."

Dunark's eyes widened at the amount mentioned, in spite of his knowledge of Earthly conditions. He started to say something, then stopped in confusion, but Seaton knew his thought.

"Sure, we can let you have thirty pounds or so; can't we, Mart?"

"Certainly. In view of what they are doing for us, I'd insist on it."

Dunark acknowledged the gift with shining eyes and heartfelt, but not profuse, thanks. He himself carried the precious stuff, escorted by a small army of commissioned officers, to the palace. He returned with a full construction crew; and, after making sure that the power-bar would work as well through arenak as through steel, he fired machine-gun-like instructions at the several foremen, then turned again to Seaton.

"Just one more thing and the men can begin. How thick do you want the walls? Our battleships carry one inch. We can't make it any thicker for lack of salt. But you have salt to give away; and, since we're doing this by an exact-copy process, I'd suggest four feet, same as you have now, to save a lot of time in making drawings and redesigning your gun-mounts and so on."

"I see. Not that we'll ever need it . . . but it would save a lot of time . . . and besides, we're used to it. Go ahead."

Dunark issued more orders. Then, as the mechanics set to work without a useless motion, he stood silent, immersed in thought.

"Worrying about Mardonale, Dunark?"

"Yes. I can't help thinking about that new weapon, whatever it is, that Nalboon now has."

"Why not build another ship, exactly like this one you're

building, with four feet of arenak, and simply blow Mardonale off the map?"

"Building the ship would be easy enough, but X is completely unknown. In fact, as you know, it cannot exist here."

"You'd have to be ungodly careful with it, that's sure. But
we've got a lot of it—we can give you a chunk of it."

"I could not accept it. It isn't like the salt."

"Sure it is. We can get a million tons of it any time we
want it." He carried one of the lumps to the airlock and
tossed it out upon the dock. "Take this nugget and get busy."

Seaton watched, entranced, as the Kondalian mechanics
set to work with skills and with tools undreamed-of on Earth.
The whole interior of the vessel was supported by a complex
falsework; then the plates and members were cut away as
though they were made of paper. The sphere, grooved for the
repellors and with the columns and central machinery complete, was molded of a stiff, plastic substance. This soon
hardened into a rocklike mass, into which all necessary openings were carefully cut.

Then the structure was washed with a very dilute solution
of salt, by special experts who took extreme pains not to lose
or waste any fraction of a drop. Platinum plates were clamped
into place and silver cables as large as a man's leg were run
to the terminals of a tight-beam power station. Current was
applied and the mass became almost invisible, transformed
into transparent arenak.

Then indeed the Earth people had a vehicle such as had
never been seen before. A four-foot shell of a substance five
hundred times as strong and hard as the strongest and hardest
steel, cast in one piece with the sustaining framework designed
by the world's foremost engineer—a structure that no conceivable force could injure, housing inconceivable force!

The falsework was removed. Columns, members, and braces
were painted black, to render them plainly visible. The walls
of the cabins were also painted, several areas being left transparent to serve as windows.

The second period of work was drawing to a close, and
Seaton and Crane both marveled at what had been accomplished.

"Both vessels will be finished tomorrow, except for the instruments and so on for ours. Another crew will work during
the sleeping-period, installing the guns and fittings."

Since the wedding was to be before fourth-meal, all three
went back to the palace, Crane and Seaton to get dressed,
Dunark to make sure that everything was as it should be.

Seaton went into Crane's room, accompanied by an attendant carrying his suitcase.

"No dress suits—shame on you!" Seaton chided. "I thought you'd thought of everything. You're slipping, little chum."

"I'm afraid so," Crane agreed, equably. "You covered it very nicely, though. Congratulations on your quick thinking. Only Dunark will know that whites are not our most formal dress."

"And he won't tell," Seaton said.

Dunark came in some time later.

"Give us a look," Seaton begged. "See if we pass inspection. I was never so rattled in my life; and the more I think about this brainstorm I had about wearing whites the less I think of it . . . but can't think of anything else we've got that would look half as good."

They were clad in spotless white, from tennis shoes to open collars. The two tall figures—Crane's slender, wiry, at perfect ease; Seaton's, broad-shouldered, powerful, prowling about with unconscious suppleness and grace—and the two high-bred faces, each wearing a look of keen anticipation, fully justified Dunark's answer.

"You'll do, fellows, and I'm not just chomping my choppers, either." With Seaton's own impulsive good-will he shook hands with them both and wished them an eternity of happiness.

"The next item on the agenda is for you to talk with your brides. . . ."

"Before the ceremony?" Seaton asked.

"Yes. This cannot be waived. You take them . . . No, you don't. That's one detail I missed. You—especially the girls—would think our formal procedure at this point somewhat indec . . . anyway, not quite nice in public. You put your arms around them and kiss them, is all. Come on."

Dorothy and Margaret had been dressed in their bridal gowns by Dunark's six wives, under the watchful eyes of his mother, the First Karfedir herself. Sitar stood the two side by side, then drew off to survey the effect.

"You are the loveliest things in the whole world!" she cried.

"Except for this horrible light," Dorothy mourned. "I wish they could see what we really look like—I'd like to, myself."

There was a peal of delighted laughter from Sitar and she spoke to one of the maids, who drew dark curtains over the windows and pressed a switch, flooding the room with pure white light.

"Dunark made these lamps," Sitar said, with intense satisfaction. "I knew exactly how you'd feel."

The two Earthmen and Dunark came in. For moments nothing was said. Seaton stared at Dorothy, hungrily and almost doubting his eyes. For white was white, pink was pink, and her gorgeous hair shone in all its natural splendor of burnished bronze.

In their wondrous Kondalian bridal costumes the girls were beautiful indeed. They wore heavily-jeweled slippers, above which were tiered anklets, each a glaze of gems. Their arms and throats were so covered with sparkling, scintillating bracelets, necklaces, and pendants that little bare skin was to be seen. And the gowns!

They were softly shimmering garments infinitely more supple than the finest silk, thick-woven of metallic threads of a fineness unknown to Earth, garments that floated about or clung to those beautifully-curved bodies in lines of exquisite grace.

For black-haired Margaret, with her ivory skin, the Kondalian princess had chosen an almost-white metal, upon which, in complicated figures, sparkled numberless jewels of pastel shades. Dorothy's gown was of a dark and lustrous green, its fabric half hidden by an intricate design of blazing green and flaming crimson gems—the strange, luminous jewels of this strange world.

Each wore her long, heavy hair almost unbound, after the Kondalian bridal fashion: brushed until it fell like a shining mist, confined only from temple to temple by a structure of jewels in rare-metal filigree.

Seaton looked from Dorothy to Margaret, then back to Dorothy. He looked into violet eyes, deep with wonder and with love, more beautiful that any jewels in all her gorgeous costume. Disregarding the notables who had been filing into the room, she placed her hands on his shoulders; he placed his on her smoothly rounded hips.

"I love you, Dick. Now and always," she said, and her own violin had no more wonderful tones than did her voice.

"I love you, Dot. Now and always," he replied; and then they both forgot all about protocol; but the demonstration apparently satisfied Kondalian requirements.

Dorothy, eyes shining, drew herself away from Seaton and glanced at Margaret.

"Isn't she the most *beautiful* thing you ever laid eyes on?"

"She certainly is not—but I'll let Mart keep on thinking she is."

Accompanied by the emperor and his son, Seaton and Crane went into the chapel which, already brilliant, had been

decorated anew with even greater splendor. Through wide
arches the Earthmen saw for the first time Osnomians wearing clothing; the great room was filled with the highest nobility of Kondal, wearing their resplendent robes of state.

As the men entered one door Dorothy and Margaret, with
the empress and Sitar, entered the other. The assemblage rose
to its feet and snapped into the grand salute. Martial music
crashed and the two parties marched toward each other, meeting at a raised platform on which stood the Karbix Tarnan, a
handsome, stately man who carried easily his eighty years of
age. Tarnan raised both arms; the music ceased.

It was a solemn and impressive spectacle. The room of burnished metal with its bizarre decorations, the constantly-
changing harmony of color from invisible lamps, the group of
nobles standing rigidly at attention in an utter absence of all
sound as the karbix lifted his arms in invocation of the First
Cause—all these things deepened the solemnity of that solemn
moment.

When Tarnan spoke, his voice, deep with some great feeling inexplicable even to those who knew him best, carried
clearly to every part of the great chamber.

"Friends, it is our privilege today to assist in a most notable
event, the marriage of four personages from another world.
For the first time in the history of Osnome has one karfedix
the honor of entertaining the bridal party of another. It is
not for this fact alone, however, that this occasion is to be
memorable. A far deeper reason is that we are witnessing,
possibly for the first time in the history of the universe, the
meeting upon terms of mutual fellowship and understanding
of the inhabitants of two worlds separated by unthinkable
distances of trackless space and by equally great differences in
evolution, conditions of life, and environment. Yet these
strangers are actuated by the spirit of good faith and honor
which is instilled into every worthy being by the great First
Cause, in the working out of whose vast projects all things are
humble instruments.

"In honor of the friendship of the two worlds, we will
proceed with the ceremony.

"Richard Seaton and Martin Crane, exchange plain rings
with Dorothy Vaneman and Margaret Spencer."

They did so, and repeated, after the karbix, simple vows
of love and loyalty.

"May the First Cause smile upon this temporary marriage
and render it worthy of permanence. As a servant and agent
of the First Cause I pronounce you two and you two husband

and wife. But we must remember that the dull vision of mortal man cannot pierce the veil of the future which is as crystal to the all-beholding eyes of the First Cause. Though you love each other truly some unforeseen thing may come between you to mar the perfection of your happiness. Therefore a time is granted you during which you will discover whether or not your unions are perfect."

After a pause Tarnan went on.

"Martin Crane, Margaret Spencer, Richard Seaton, Dorothy Vaneman: you are before us to take the final vows which will bind your bodies together for life and your spirits together for eternity. Have you considered the gravity of this step sufficiently to enter into this marriage without reservation?"

"I have," the four replied in unison.

"Don, for a moment, the helmets before you."

They did so, and upon each of four oscilloscope screens there appeared hundreds of irregular lines. Dead silence held while Tarnan studied certain traces upon each of the four giant screen, which were plainly visible to everyone in the room.

"I have seen—each man and woman of this congregation has seen—that each one of you four visiting personages is of the evolutionary state required for eternal marriage. Remove the helmets. . . . exchange the jeweled rings. Do you each individually swear, in the presence of the First Cause and before the supreme justices of Kondal, that you will be true and loyal, each helping his chosen one in all things, great and small; that never, throughout eternity, in thought or in action, will your mind or your body or your spirit stray from the path of truth and honor?"

"I do."

"I pronounce you married with the eternal marriage. Just as the faidon which each of you wears—the eternal jewel which no force of man is able to change or to deform and which gives off its inward light without change and without end—shall endure through endless cycles of time after the metal of the ring that holds it shall have crumbled in decay: even so shall your spirits, formerly two, now one and indissoluble, progress in ever-ascending evolution throughout eternity after the base material which is your bodies shall have commingled with the base material from which it came."

The karbix lowered his arms and the bridal party walked to the door through ranks of uplifted weapons. They were led to another room, where the contracting parties signed their names in a register. Dunark then produced two marriage certificates—plates of a brilliant purple metal, beautifully engraved in parallel columns of English and Kondalian script and heavily bordered with precious stones. The principals and witnesses signed below each column and the signatures were engraved into the metal.

They were then escorted to the dining hall, where a truly royal repast was served. Between courses the nobles welcomed the visitors and wished them happiness. After the last course Tarnan spoke, his voice again agitated by the emotion that had puzzled his hearers during the marriage service.

"All Kondal is with us here in spirit, joining us in welcoming these our guests, of whose friendship no greater warrant could be given than their willingness to grant us the privilege of their marriage. Not only have they given us a boon that will make their names revered throughout the nation as long as Kondal shall exist, but also they have been the means of showing us plainly that the First Cause is upon our side; that our ages-old institution of honor is in truth the only foundation upon which can be built a race worthy to survive. At the same time they have been the means of showing us that our hated foe, entirely without honor, building his race upon a foundation of bloodthirsty savagery alone, is building wrongly and must perish utterly from the face of Osnome."

His hearers listened, impressed by his earnestness, but not understanding his meaning, and he went on, with a deep light shining in his eyes.

"You do not understand? It is inevitable that two peoples as different as are our two should be possessed of widely-differing knowledges and abilities. These friends, from their remote world, have already made it possible for us to construct engines of destruction which will obliterate Mardonale completely—"

A fierce shout of joy interrupted the speaker and the nobles sprang to their feet, saluting the visitors with weapons held aloft. As soon as they had reseated themselves Tarnan went on.

"That is the boon. The vindication of our evolution is as easily explained. These friends landed first in Mardonale. Had Nalboon met them in honor, he would have gained the boon. But he attempted to kill his guests and steal their treasures, with what results you already know. We, however, in exchange for the few and trifling services we have been able to render them, have received even more of value than Nalboon

would have obtained, even had his plans not been nullified
by their vastly higher state of evolution."

There was a clamor of cheering as Tarnan sat down. The
nobles formed themselves into an escort of honor and con-
ducted the two couples to their apartments.

Alone in one of their rooms, Dorothy turned to her husband with tears shining in her eyes.

"Dick, sweetheart, wasn't that the most wonderful thing
you ever heard of? Grand, in the old meaning of the word—
really grand. And that old man was simply superb. I'll never
get over it."

"It was all of that, Dot. It got down to where I lived.
So much so that I stopped having the jitters as soon as it
started."

But, manlike, Seaton had had enough of solemnity for one
day. "But do you know that I haven't had a good look at you
yet, under light I can see by? Stand over there, beautiful, and
let me feast my eyes."

"I will not." She responded instantly to his mood. "I
haven't seen myself, either, and that's just as important . . ."

"More so," he said, with a wide and happy smile. "So we'll
go over to that full-length mirror and both feast our eyes."

"Of course I saw Peggy, for about a second, but I can't
tell much from that. She's su—" She broke off in the middle
of a one-syllable word and stared into the mirror.

"That," she gasped, "is me? I, I mean? Dorothy Vaneman
—I mean Seaton?"

"That is Dorothy Seaton," he assured her. "Yes. Irrevocably
so."

She stuck out a foot, the better to examine the slipper. She
lifted her gown well above her knees and studied anklets and
legbands. She put her hands on her hips and wriggled, setting
everything above the waist into motion. She turned around
and repeated the performance, to watch the ornaments dance
on her far-from-niggardly expanse of back. She studied the
towering, fantastically-jeweled headdress. Then she turned to
Seaton, sheer delight spreading over her expressive face.

"You know what, Dick?" she exclaimed, gleefully. "I'm
going to wear this whole regalia, just exactly as it is, to the
President's Ball!"

"You wouldn't. You couldn't. Nobody could have that
much nerve."

"That's what you think. But you aren't a woman—thanks
be! Just wait and see. You know that red-headed copy-cat,
Maribel Whitcomb?"

"I've heard you mention her—unfavorably."

"Just wait 'til she sees *this*, the be-hennaed, be-padded vixen! Her eyes will stick out as though they had stalks, and she'll die of envy and frustration right there on the floor—she can't even try to copy this!"

"Check—to even more than the proverbial nineteen decimals. But we've got to change, or we'll be late."

"Uh-huh, I suppose so." Dorothy kept on looking backward at the mirror as they walked away. "One thing's sure, though, Dickie mine. I don't know about the 'deafening report' part, but I certainly am a blinding flash!"

chapter **20**

"THESE JEWELS PUZZLE ME, DICK. WHAT ARE they?" Crane asked, as the four assembled, waiting for first-meal. He held up his third finger, upon which gleamed the royal jewel of Kondal in its mounting of intensely blue transparent arenak. "I know the name, faidon, but that is about all I seem to know."

"That's about all anybody knows. It occurs naturally just as you see it there—deep blue, apparently but not actually transparent, constantly emitting that strong blue light. It cannot be worked, cut, ground, or even scratched. It will not burn or change in any arc Kondalians can generate—and believe you me, that's saying a mouthful. It doesn't change in liquid helium. In other words, Mart, it seems to be inert."

"How about acids?"

"I've been wondering about that. And fusion mixtures and such. Osnomians are pretty far back in chemistry. I'm going to get hold of another one and see if I can't break it down, some way or other. I can't seem to convince myself that an atomic structure could be that big."

"No, it would be a trifle oversize for an atom." Crane turned to the two girls. "How do you like your solitaires?"

"They're perfectly beautiful, and this Tiffany mounting is exquisite," Dorothy replied, enthusiastically. "But they're so awfully big. They're as big as ten-carat diamonds, I do believe."

"Just about," Seaton said, "but at that, they're the smallest Dunark could find. They've been kicking around for years, he says, so small nobody wanted them. They like big ones, you know. Wait until you get back to Washington, Dot. People will think you're wearing a bottle-stopper until they see it shining in the dark, and then they'll think it's a misplaced taillight. But when the news gets out—wow! Jewelers will be bidding up, a million bucks per jump, for rich old dames who want something nobody else can get. Check?"

"You are right, Dick," Crane said, thoughtfully. "Since we intend to wear them continuously, jewelers will see them. Any jewel expert will know at a glance that they are new, unique, and fabulously valuable. In fact, they could get us into serious trouble, as fabulous jewels do."

"Yeah . . . I never thought of that . . . well, how about this? We'll let it out, casual-like, that they're as common as mud up here. That we're wearing them purely for sentiment—that, at least, will be true—and we're going to bring in a shipload of 'em to sell for everlasting, no-battery-needed, automobile parking lamps. And if our girl friends really do wear their gowns to the President's Ball, as Dot says they're going to, that'll help, too. Nobody—but nobody—would wear thirty-eight pounds of cut stones on a dress if they cost very much per each."

"That would probably keep anyone from murdering our wives for their rings, at least."

"Have you read your marriage certificate, Dick?" Margaret asked.

"No. Let's look at it, Dottie."

She produced the massive, heavily-jeweled document, and the auburn head and the brown one were very close to each other as they read together the English side of the certificate. Their vows were there, word for word, with their own signatures beneath them, all deeply engraved into the metal. Seaton smiled as he saw the legal form engraved below the signatures, and read aloud:

"*I, the head of the church and the commander-in-chief of the armed forces of Kondal, upon the planet Osnome, certify that I have this day, in the city of Kondalek, of said nation and planet, joined in indissoluble bonds of matrimony, Richard Ballinger Seaton, Doctor of Philosophy, and Dorothy Lee Vaneman, Doctor of Music; both of Washington, D.C., U.S.A., upon the planet Earth, in strict compliance with the marriage laws, both of Kondal and of the District of Columbia.*"

"Tarnan, Karbix of Kondal

"Witnesses:
   Roban, Emperor of Kondal.
   Tural, Empress of Kondal.
   Dunark, Crown Prince of Kondal.
   Sitar, Crown Princess of Kondal.
   Marc C. DuQuesne, Washington, D.C., U.S.A.,
      Earth."

"That's some document," Seaton said. "How'd he know it complies with the marriage laws of the District? I'm wondering if it does. 'Indissoluble' and 'eternity' are mighty big words for American marriages. Do you think we'd better get married again when we get back?"

Both girls protested vigorously and Crane said, "No, I think not. I intend to register this just as it is and get a court ruling on it. It will undoubtedly prove legal."

"I'm not too sure about that," Seaton argued. "Is there any precedent in law that says a man can make a promise that will be binding on his immortal soul for all the rest of eternity?"

"I rather doubt it. I'm sure there will be, however, when our attorneys close the case. You forget, Dick, that The Seaton-Crane Company, Engineers has a very good legal staff."

"That's right, I had. I'll bet they'll have fun, kicking that one around. I wish that bell would ring."

"So do I," Dorothy said. "I just can't get used to not having any night, and . . ."

"And it's such a long time between meals," Seaton put in, "as the two famous governors said about the drinks."

"How did you know what I was going to say?"

"Husbandly intuition," he grinned, "aided and abetted by a stomach that is accustomed to only six hours between eats."

After eating, the men hurried to the Skylark. During the sleeping-period the repellors had been banded on and the guns and instruments, including a full Kondalian radio system, had been installed. Except for the power-bars, she was ready to fly. The Kondalian vessel lacked both power-bars and instruments.

"How's the copper situation, Dunark?" Seaton asked.

"I don't know yet, exactly. Crews are out, scouring the city for all the metallic copper they can find, but they won't find very much. As you know, we don't use it, as platinum, iridium, silver, and gold are so much better for ordinary use. We're working full time on the copper plant, but it'll be a day or so yet before we can produce virgin copper. I'm going to work on our instruments and controls—if you two are temporarily at a loose end, you might help me."

Both men were glad to be of assistance; Crane was delighted at the chance to learn how to work that very hard and extremely stubborn metal, iridium, from which all the Kondalian instruments were to be made.

On the way to the instrument shop Seaton said to Crane, "But what tickles me most is this arenak; and not only for armor and so forth. I s'pose you've noticed your razor?"

"How could I help it?"

"I can't understand how anything can be that hard, Mart. Forty years on an arenak-dust abrasive machine—diamond-dust won't touch it—to hone it, and then it'll shave ten men every day for a thousand years and still have exactly the same edge it started with. That is what I would call a contribution to science."

Dunark's extraordinary skill and his even more extraordinary automatic machine tools made the manufacture of his instruments a comparatively short job. While it was going on, the foreman in charge of the scrap-copper drive came in to report. Enough had been found to make two bars, with a few pounds to spare. The bars were in the engines, one in each ship.

"Well done, Kolanix Melnen," Dunark said, warmly. "I didn't expect nearly that much."

"We got every last bit of metallic copper in the whole city," the foreman said, proudly.

"Fine!" Seaton applauded. "With one bar apiece, we're ready. Let 'em come."

"We don't want them to come here; we want to go there," Dunark said. "One bar apiece isn't enough for that."

"That's right," Seaton agreed. "For an invasion in force, no. I'd let you have ours, but two wouldn't be any better than one."

"No. Four, at least, and I'm going to have eight. There should be some way of speeding up work on that copper plant, but I haven't been able to think of any."

"Speed it up? It's going at fantastic speed already. On Earth it takes months, not days, to build smelters and refineries."

"I've got half a notion to go over there . . . but . . ."

" 'But' is right." Seaton said. "You'd be more apt to throw the boys off stride than anything else."

"Could be . . . but . . ."

"*The Karlon was hurled backward to the point of equilibrium of the two forces, where it struggled demoniacally.*"

While the Kondalian prince was still standing, undecided, a call for help came in. A freight-plane was being pursued by a karlon a few hundred miles away.

"Now's your time to study one, Dunark!" Seaton exclaimed. "We'll drag him in here—get your scientists out here!"

The *Skylark* reached the monster before it reached the freighter. Seaton focused the attractor and threw on power, jerking the beast upward and backward. As it saw the puny size of the *Skylark* it opened its cavernous mouth and rushed to attack. Seaton, not wishing to have his ship stripped of repellors, turned them on. The monster was hurled backward to the point of equilibrium of the two forces, where it hung helpless, struggling frantically.

Seaton towed the captive back to the field. By judicious pushing and pulling, and by using every attractor and repellor the *Skylark* mounted, the three Earthmen finally managed to hold that monstrous body flat on the ground; but not even with the help of Dunark's vessel could all of the terrible tentacles be pinned down. The scientists studied the creature as well as they could, from battleships and from heavily-armored tanks.

"I wish we could kill it without blowing it to bits," said Dunark, via radio. "Do you know of any way of doing it?"

"No—except maybe poison. And since we don't know what would poison it, and couldn't make it if we did, I don't see much chance. Maybe we can tire him out, though, and find out where he lives."

After the scholars had learned all they could, Seaton yanked the animal a few miles into the air and shut off the forces holding it. There was a crash and the karlon, knowing that this apparently insignificant vessel was its master, shot away in headlong flight.

"What was that noise, Dick?" Crane asked.

"I don't know—a new one on me. Probaby we cracked a few of his plates," Seaton replied, as he drove the *Skylark* after the monster.

Pitted for the first time in its life against an antagonist who could both outfly and outfight it, the karlon put everything it had into its giant wings. It flew back over the city of Kondalek, over the outlying country, and out over the ocean. As they neared the Mardonalian border a fleet of warships came up to meet the monster; and Seaton, not wanting to let the enemy see the rejuvenated *Skylark* too closely, jerked the captive high into the air. It headed for the ocean in a perpendicular dive. Seaton focused an object-compass upon it.

"Go to it, sport," he said. "We'll follow you clear to the bottom, if you want to go that far!"

There was a tremendous double splash as pursued and pursuer struck the water. Dorothy gasped, seized a hand-hold, and shut both eyes; but she could scarcely feel the shock, so tremendous was the strength of the *Sklark's* new hull and so enormous the power that drove her. Seaton turned on his searchlights and closed in. Deeper and deeper the quarry dove; it became clear that the thing was just as much at home in the water as it was in the air.

The lights revealed strange forms of life, among which were staring-eyed fishes, floundering blindly in the unaccustomed glare. As the karlon bored still deeper the living things became scarcer; but the Earthmen still saw from time to time the living nightmares that inhabited the oppressive depths of those strange seas. Continuing downward, the karlon went clear to the bottom and stopped there, stirring up a murk of ooze.

"How deep are we, Mart?"

"Something under four miles. No fine figures yet."

"Of course not. Strain gauges okay?"

"Scarcely moved off their zeroes."

"Ha! Good news, even though I knew—with my mind— that they wouldn't. With our steel hull they'd've been 'way up in the red. Wonderful stuff, this arenak. Well, it looks as though he wants to sit it out here and we won't find out anything that way. Come on, sport, let's go somewhere else!" Spaceship and karlon went straight up—fast.

On reaching the surface, the monster decided to grab altitude, and went so high that Seaton was amazed.

"I wouldn't have believed that such a thing could possibly fly in air so thin!" he exclaimed.

"It is thin up here," Crane said. "Four point one six pounds per square inch."

"This is his ceiling, I guess. Wonder what he'll do next?"

As if in answer the karlon dived toward the lowlands of Kondal, a swampy region lush with poisonous vegetation and inhabited only by venomous reptiles. As it approached the surface Seaton slowed the *Skylark* down, remarking, "He'll have to flatten out pretty quick or he'll bust something."

But it did not flatten out. Diving all out, it struck the morass head-first and disappeared.

Astonished at such an un-looked-for development, Seaton

brought the Skylark to a halt and stabbed downward with the full power of the attractor. The first stab brought up nothing but a pillar of muck; the second, one wing and one arm; the third, the whole animal—fighting as savagely as ever.

Seaton eased the attractor's grip. "If he digs in here again we'll follow him."

"Will the ship stand it?" DuQuesne asked.

"She'll stand anything. But you'd better all hang on. I don't know whether there'll be much of a jar or not."

There was scarcely any jar at all. After the Skylark had been pulling herself downward, quite effortlessly, for something over one minute, Seaton glanced across at Crane; who was sitting still at his board doing nothing at all except smiling quietly to himself.

"What're you grinning about, you Cheshire cat?"

"Just wondering what you came down here for and what you're going to prove. These instruments are lying, unanimously and enthusiastically. Plastic flow, you know, not fluid."

"Oh . . . uh-huh, check. No lights, radar, or . . . We could build a sounder, though, or a velocitometer."

"There are quite a few things we can do, if you think it worth while to take the time."

"It isn't, of course."

After a few minutes more, Seaton again hauled the monster to the surface and into the air. Again it attacked, with unabated fury.

"Well, that's about enough of that, I guess. Apparently he isn't going home—unless his home was down there in the mud, which I can't quite believe. We can't waste much more time, so you might as well put him away."

The Mark Five struck; the ground rocked and heaved under the concussion.

"Hey, I just thought of something!" Seaton exclaimed. "We could have taken him out and set him into an orbit around the planet. Without air, water, or food he'd die sometime—I think. Then they'd have a perfect specimen to study."

"Why, Dick, what a horrible idea!" Dorothy's eyes flashed as she turned on him. "You wouldn't want even such a monster as that to die that way!"

"No, I guess I wouldn't really. He's a game fighter. So we'll let Dunark do it sometime, if he wants to."

The Skylark reached the palace dock just before fourth-meal, and while they were all eating Dunark told Seaton that the copper plant would be in production in a few hours, and that the first finished bar would roll at point thirty-four—in other words, immediately after first-meal of the following "day."

"Fine!" Seaton exclaimed. "You'll be ready in the *Kondal*. Take the first eight bars and be on your way. F-f-f-f-t! There goes Mardonale!"

"Impossible, as you already know, if you think a little."

"Oh . . . I see . . . the Code. I wouldn't want you to break it, of course . . . but couldn't it be . . . say, stretched just enough to cover a situation like this, which has never come up before?"

"It can not." Dunark said, stiffly.

"But s'pose . . . Pardon me, Dunark. Ignorance—I never really scanned it before. You're right. I'll play ball."

" 'Smatter, Dick?" Dorothy whispered into his ear. "What did you do to him? I thought he was going to blow his top."

"I said something I should have known better than to say," he replied, loudly enough so that Dunark, too, could hear. "Also, I shouldn't have told you the schedule I had in mind. It's been changed. The *Skylark* gets her copper first, then the *Kondal*. And Dunark doesn't leave until we do. Why, I don't know, any more than Dunark can figure out, with all he got from my mind, why you and I insist on wearing clothes. A matter of code."

"But, just that little extra time wouldn't make any difference, would it?"

"One chance in a million, maybe, with the bars rolling off the line so fast—no, after all this time, half an hour more won't make any difference. I suppose your men are loading the platinum, Dunark."

"Yes. They're filling Number Three storeroom full."

"Good work, Seaton," DuQuesne said. "I've often wished there was some way of getting platinum out of jewelry and into laboratories and production, and your scheme will do it. I don't think much of your judgment in passing up the chance to make a million bucks or so, but I'll be glad to see jewelers drop platinum. I wonder how they'll put it across that platinum isn't the thing for jewelry any more?"

"Oh, they can keep on using it, all they want of it," Seaton said, innocently, "at exactly the same price as stainless steel."

"Who do you think you're kidding?" DuQuesne's reply was not a question, but a sneer.

On the following "morning," immediately after "breakfast," enough bars were ready to supply both vessels. The

Skylark was fueled first, then the *Kondal*. Both ships hopped across plain and city and, timed to the split second, landed as one upon the palace dock. Both crews disembarked and stood at half-attention, the three Americans dressed in their whites, the twenty Kondalian high officers wearing their robes of state.

"This stuff is for the birds." Seaton's lips scarcely moved, only Crane could hear him. "We stand here for exactly so many seconds, to give the natives a treat." His eyes flicked upward at the aircraft filling the air. "Then we come to full attention as the grand moguls and high panjandrums appear, escorting our wives, and the battleships salute, and—blast such flummery!"

"But think of how the girls are enjoying it." Crane said, using Seaton's own technique. "And you are going to do it, so why gripe about it?"

"I'd like to do more than pop off—I'd like to call Dot and tell her to shake a leg—but I won't. With Dunark what he is I have to play ball, but I don't have to like it."

chapter **21**

SUDDENLY THE SILENCE WAS SHATTERED. Bells rang, sirens shrieked, whistles screamed, every radio and visiset and communicator in or near the city of Kondalek began to clamor. All were giving the same dire warning, the alarm extraordinary of invasion, of imminent and catastrophic danger from the air. Seaton leaped toward the nearest elevator, but whirled back toward the *Skylark* even before Dunark spoke.

"Don't try it, Dick—you can't possibly make it. Everyone will have time to reach the bomb-proofs. They'll be safe—if we can keep the Mardonalians from landing."

"They won't land—except in hell." The three sprang into the *Skylark;* Seaton going to the board, Crane and DuQuesne to the guns. Crane picked up his microphone.

"Send in English, and tell the girls not to answer," Seaton directed. "They can locate calls to a foot. Just tell 'em we're safe and to sit tight while we wipe out this gang of highbinders that's coming."

DuQuesne was breaking out box after box of belts of ammunition. "What do you want first, Seaton? There's not enough of any one load to fight much of a battle."

"Start with Mark Fives and go up to Tens. That ought to be enough. If not, follow up with Fours and so on down."

"Fives to Tens; Fours and down. Check."

There was a crescendo whine of enormous propellers, followed by a concussion of sound as one wing of the palace disappeared in a cloud of dust and debris.

The air was full of Mardonalian warships. They were huge vessels, each mounting hundreds of guns; and a rain of high-explosive shells was reducing the entire city to ruins.

"Hold it!" Seaton's hand, already on the lever, was checked. "Look at the *Kondal*—something's up!"

Dunark sat at his board and every man of his crew was at his station; but all were writhing in agony, completely unable to control their movements. As Seaton finished speaking the Kondalians ceased their agonized struggling and hung, unconscious or dead, from whatever each was holding.

"They've got to them some way—let's go!" Seaton yelled.

The dock beneath them fell apart and all three men thought the end of the world had come as a stream of shells struck the *Skylark* and exploded. But that four-foot armor of arenak was impregnable and Seaton lifted his ship upward, directly into the Mardonalian fleet. DuQuesne and Crane fired carefully; as rapidly as each could, consistent with making every bullet count; and as each bullet struck a warship disappeared and there erupted a blast of noise in which the explosions of the Mardonalian shells, violent as they were, were completely inaudible.

"You haven't got the repellors on, Dick!" Crane snapped.

"No, dammit—what a brain!" He snapped them on, then, as the unbearable din subsided almost to a murmur, he shouted, "Hey! They must be repelling even most of the air!"

The *Skylark* was now being attacked by every ship of the Mardonalian fleet, every unit having been diverted from its mission of destruction to the task of wiping out this appallingly deadly, apallingly invulnerable midget.

From every point of the compass, from above and below, came torrents of shells. Nor were there shells alone. There came also guided missiles—tight-beam-radio-steered airplane-torpedoes—carrying warheads of fantastic power. But none of them struck arenak. Instead, they all struck an immaterial wall of pure force and exploded a hundred feet off target, creating an almost continuous glare of fury and flame.

And Crane and DuQuesne kept on firing. Half of the invading fleet had been destroyed and they were now using Mark Sixes and Mark Sevens—and anything struck by a Seven was not merely blown to bits. It was comminuted—disintegrated—volatilized—almost dematerialized.

Suddenly the shelling stopped and the Skylark was enveloped in a blinding glare from a thousand projectors; an intense, searching, violet light that would burn flesh and sear its way through eyelids and eyeballs into the very brain.

"Shut your eyes!" Seaton yelled as he shoved the lever forward. "Turn your heads!"

Then they were out in space. "That's pretty nearly atomic-bomb flash," DuQuesne said, incredulously. "How can they generate that kind of stuff here?"

"I don't know," Seaton said, "But that isn't the question. What can we do about it?"

The three talked briefly, then put on space-suits, which they smeared liberally with thick red paint. Under their helmets they wore extra-heavy welding goggles, so dark in color as to be almost black.

"This'll stop *that* kind of monkey business," Seaton exulted, as he again threw the Skylark into the Mardonalian fleet.

It took about fifteen seconds for the enemy to get their projectors focused, during which time some twenty battleships were volatilized; but this time the killing light was not alone.

The men heard, or rather felt, a low, intense vibration, like a silent wave of sound, a vibration which smote upon the eardrums as no possible sound could smite, a vibration that racked the joints and tortured the nerves as though the whole body were being disintegrated. So sudden and terrible was the effect that Seaton uttered an involuntary yelp of surprise and pain as he once more fled to the safety of space.

"What the devil was that?" DuQuesne demanded. "Can they generate and project infra-sound?"

"Yes." Seaton replied. "They can do a lot of things that we can't."

"If we had some fur suits . . ." Crane began, then paused. "Put on all the clothes we can, and use ear-plugs?"

"We can do better than that, I think." Seaton studied his board. "I'll short out this resistor, so as to put more juice through the repellors. I can get a pretty good vacuum that way; certainly good enough to stop any wave propagated through air."

Back within range of the enemy, DuQuesne, reaching for his gun, leaped away from it with a yell. "Beat it!"

Once more at a safe distance, DuQuesne explained.

"That gun had voltage, and plenty of it. It's lucky that I'm so used to handling hot stuff that I never really make contact with anything at first touch. That's easy, though. Thick, dry gloves and rubber shields is all we need. It's a good thing for all of us that you have those fancy handles on your levers, Seaton."

"That must have been how they got Dunark and his crew. But why didn't they get you two then? Oh, I see. They had it tuned to iridium. They don't know anything about steel—unless they chipped a sample off somewhere—so it took them until now to tune to it."

"You recognize everything that hapens," Crane said. "Can you tell what they're going to do next?"

"Not quite everything. This last one was new—it must be the big new one Dunark was worrying about. The others, yes; but the defenses against them are purely Kondalian in technique and material, so we have to roll our own as we go. As to what's coming next . . ." He paused in thought, then went on, "I wish I knew. You see, I got too many new things at once, so most of them are like dimly-remembered things that flash into real knowledge only when they happen. But maybe mentioning something would do the trick. Let's see . . . what have they given us so far?"

"They've given us plenty," DuQuesne said, admiringly. "Light, ultra and visible; sound, infra- or sub-sound; and solid jolts of high-tension electricity. They haven't yet used X-rays, accelerated particles, Hertzian waves, infra-red heat . . ."

"That's it—heat!" Seaton exclaimed. "They project a wave that sets up induced currents in arenak. They can melt armor that way—given time enough."

"Our refrigerators can handle a lot of heat." Crane said.

"They certainly can . . . the limit being the amount of water on board . . . and when we run out of water we can hop over to the ocean and cool the shell off. Are we ready?"

They were, and soon the *Skylark* was again dealing out death and destruction to the enemy vessels, who again turned from the devastation of the helpless city to destroy this tiny, but incredibly powerful antagonist. And DuQuesne, considerably the faster of the two gunners, was now shooting Mark Tens—and in the starkly incomprehensible violence of those earth-shaking blasts ten or twelve battleships usually went into their component atoms instead of only two or three.

After only a few minutes the *Skylark*'s armor began to heat up and Seaton turned the refrigerators, already operating at full rating, up to the absolute top of fifty per cent overload. Even that was not enough. Although the interior of the ship stayed comfortably cool, the armor was so thick that it simply could not conduct heat fast enough. The outer layers grew hotter and hotter—red, cherry red, white. The ends of the rifle barrels, set flush with the surfaces of the arenak globes holding them, began to soften and to melt, so that firing became impossible. The copper repellors began to melt and to drip away in flaming droplets, so that exploding shells and missiles came closer and closer.

"Well, it looks as though they have us stopped for the moment," DuQuesne said calmly, with no thought of quitting apparent in either voice or manner. "Let's go dope out something else."

They again went up out of range, but had only started discussing ways and means when a call came, uncoded and on the general wave.

"Karfedix Seaton——Karfedix Seaton——acknowledge, please——Karfedix Seaton——Karfed— . . . . . ."

"Seaton acknowledging!"

"This is Karfedelix Depar, commanding four task-forces. The Karbix Tarnan has ordered me to report . . ."

"He has broken radio silence, then?" Seaton demanded.

"I have." The karbix did not go on to explain, either that it was necessary or that it was now safe to do so. Seaton knew both of those facts.

"Good!" and Seaton went on to explain to both commander-in-chief and commander the nature and deadliness of Mardonale's new weapon. "Karfedelix Depar, continue your report."

"The Karbix Tarnan ordered me to report to you for orders. There is a Mardonalian fleet approaching from the east. Have I your permission, sir, to attack it?"

"Can you insulate, against twenty kilovolts, all the iridium your men must touch?"

"I think so, sir."

"Thinking so isn't enough. If you can't, land and get insulation before engaging with any Mardonalian vessel. Are any more of our task forces en route?"

"Yes, sir. Four within the quarter-hour, three more in one, two, and three hours respectively, sir."

"Report acknowledged. Stand by." Seaton frowned in thought. He had to appoint an admiral; but he certainly did not want to ask, with every living Kondalian listening, whether or not this Depar was a big enough man for the job.

"Karbix Tarnan, sir," he said.

"Tarnan acknowledging."

"Sir, which of your officers now in air is best fitted to command the defense fleet now assembling?"

"Sir, the Karfedelix Depar."

"Sir, thank you. Karfedelix Depar, I give you authority to handle and responsibility for handling correctly the forthcoming engagement. Take command!"

"Thank you, sir."

Seaton dropped his microphone. "I've got it doped," he told Crane and DuQuesne. "The Skylark's faster than any shell ever fired, and has infinitely more mass. She's got four feet of arenak, they have only an inch. Arenak doesn't begin to soften until it's radiating high in the ultra-violet. Strap down solid—this is going to be a rough party from now on."

Again the Skylark went down. Instead of standing still, however, she darted directly at the nearest warship under twenty notches of power. She crashed straight through it without even slowing down. Torn wide open by the forty-foot projectile, its engines wrecked and its helicopter-screws and propellers useless, the helpless hulk plunged through two miles of air to the ground.

Darting here and there, the spaceship tore through vessel after vessel of the Mardonalian fleet. Here indeed was a guided missile: an irresistible projectile housing a human brain, the brain of Richard Seaton, keyed up to highest pitch and fighting the fight of his life.

As the repellors dripped off, the silent waves of sound came in stronger and stronger. He was battered by the terrific impacts, nauseated and almost blacked out by the frightful lurches of his hairpin turns. Nevertheless, with teeth tight-locked and with eyes gray and hard as the fracture of high-carbon steel, Richard Seaton fought on. Projectile and brain were, and remained, one.

Although it was impossible for the eye to follow the flight of the spaceship, the mechanical sighting devices of the Mardonalians kept her in fair focus and the projectors continued to hurl into her a considerable fraction of their death-dealing output. Enemy guns were still emitting streams of shells; but, unlike the waves, the shells moved so slowly compared to their target that very few found their mark. Many

*"The 'Skylark' darted forward and crashed
completely through the great air-ship."*

of the great vessels fell to the ground, riddled by the shells of their sister-ships.

Seaton glanced at his pyrometer. The needle had stopped climbing, well short of the red line marking the fusion-point of arenak. Even as he looked, it began, very slowly, to recede. There weren't enough Mardonalian ships left to maintain such a temperature. He felt much better, too; the sub-sound was still pretty bad, but it was bearable.

In another minute the battle was over; the few remaining battleships were driving at top speed for home. But even in flight they continued to destroy; the path of their retreat was a swath of destruction. Half-inclined at first to let them escape, Seaton's mind was changed as he saw what they were doing to the countryside beneath them. He shot after them, and not until the last vessel had been destroyed did he drop the *Skylark* into the area of ruins which had once been the palace grounds, beside the *Kondal*, which was still lying as it had fallen.

After several attempts to steady their whirling senses the three men were able to walk. They opened the lock and leaped out, through the still white-hot wall. Seaton's first act was to call Dorothy, who told him that the royal party would come up as soon as engineers could clear the way. The men then removed their helmets, revealing pale and drawn faces, and turned to the *Kondal*.

"There's no way of getting into this thing. . . . Oh, fine! They're coming to!"

Dunark opened the lock and stumbled out. "I have to thank you for more than my life, this time," he said, his voice shaken as much by emotion as by the shock of his experience as he grasped the hands of all three men. "I was conscious most of the time and saw most of what happened. You have saved all Kondal."

"Oh, it's not that bad," Seaton said, uncomfortably. "Both nations have been invaded before."

"Yes, but not with anything like this. This would have been final. But I must hurry. If you will relinquish command to me, Dick, please, I will restore it to the karbix. The *Kondal* will of course be his flagship."

Seaton snapped to attention and saluted. "Kofedix Dunark, sir, I relinquish to you my command."

"Karfedix Seaton, sir, with thanks for what you have done, I accept your command."

Dunark hurried away, talking as he went with surviving officers of the grounded Kondalian warships.

In a few minutes the emperor and his party rounded a

heap of boulders. Dorothy and Margaret screamed in unison as they saw the haggard faces of their husbands and saw their suits dripping with red. Seaton dodged as Dorothy reached him, and tore off his suit.

"Nothing but red paint," he assured her, as he lifted her off the ground.

Out of the corner of his eye he saw the Kondalians staring in open-mouthed amazement at the *Skylark*. He turned. She was a huge ball of frost and snow!

As Seaton came back to the girls from shutting off the refrigerators, Roban came up and gave the Earthmen thanks in the name of his nation for what they had done.

"Has it yet occurred to you, Karfedix Roban," Margaret said, diffidently, "that, had it not been for your rigid adherence to your Code, none of us Tellurians would have been on Osnome or near it when the Mardonalians attacked you?"

"No, my daughter . . . by no means . . . I still fail to see the connection. Will you explain, please?"

"Dick's idea was to have Dunark take the first eight bars of copper and sail for Mardonale. Then we would take the next forty bars—which would take about half an hour to make—and leave immediately for Earth. Then, when Dunark arrived over Mardonale he would have been shot down out of control—wouldn't he?"

"Undoubtedly. . . . I understand now, but go ahead."

"How long did it take the Mardonalian fleet to get here, about?"

"About forty of your hours."

"Then, assuming that Dunark didn't take any time at all in getting over there, we would have been gone about thirty-nine and a half hours when they struck . . . but there wasn't that much time! They must have been well on the way while we were getting the copper!"

"Very true, daughter Margaret, but the end result would have been precisely the same. You would have been gone at least one hour—which, for us, would have been as bad as one thousand."

The Karfedix Roban stood facing the party from Earth. Back of him stood his family, the officers and nobility, and a multitude of people.

"Is it permitted, karfedo, that I award your captive some small recognition of the service he has done my nation?" Roban asked.

"It is permitted," Seaton and Crane replied, in unison; whereupon Roban stepped forward and, after handing

DuQuesne a heavy bag, fastened about his left wrist the emblem of the Order of Kondal.

"I welcome you, Karfedelix DuQuesne, to the highest nobility of Kondal."

He then clasped around Crane's wrist a bracelet of ruby-red metal bearing a peculiarly wrought, heavily-jeweled disk, at the sight of which the nobles saluted and Seaton barely concealed a start of surprise.

"Karfedix Crane, I bestow upon you this symbol; which proclaims that, throughout all Kondalian Osnome, you have authority as my personal representative in all things, great and small."

Approaching Seaton, Roban held up a bracelet of seven disks so that everyone could see it. The nobles knelt; the people prostrated themselves.

"Karfedix Seaton, no language spoken by man possesses words able to express our indebtedness to you. In small and partial recognition of that indebtedness I bestow upon you these symbols, which declare you to be our overlord, the ultimate authority upon all Osnome."

Lifting both arms above his head he continued.

"May the great First Cause smile upon you in all your endeavors until you solve the Prime Mystery; may your descendants soon reach the Ultimate Goal. Good-bye."

Seaton spoke a few heartfelt words in response and the five Earth-people stepped backward toward their ship. As they reached it the standing emperor and the ranks of nobles snapped into the double salute—truly a rare gesture.

"What'll we do now?" Seaton whispered. "I'm fresh out of ideas."

"Bow, of course," Dorothy said.

They bowed, deeply and slowly, and entered their vessel; and as the Skylark shot into the air the grand fleet of Kondalian warships fired a royal salute.

chapter **22**

DUQUESNE'S FIRST ACT UPON GAINING THE privacy of his own cabin was to open the bag presented to him by the emperor. He expected to find it filled with rare metals, with perhaps some jewels, instead of which the only metal present was in a heavily-insulated tube—a full half pound of metallic radium!

The least valuable items of his prize were hundreds of diamonds, rubies, and emeralds of very large size and of flawless perfection. Merely ornamental glass to Roban, he had known their Earthly value. To this wealth of known gems Roban had added a rich and varied assortment of the strange jewels peculiar to his own world, the faidon alone being absent from the collection. DuQuesne's calmness almost deserted him as he sorted out and listed the contents of the bag.

The radium alone was worth millions of dollars; and the scientist in him exulted at the uses to which it would be put, even while he was also exulting at the price he would get for it. He counted the familiar jewels, estimating their value as he did so—a staggering total. That left the strange gems, enough to fill the bag half full—shining and glowing and scintillating in multi-colored splendor. He sorted them out and counted them, but made no effort to appraise them. He knew that he could get any price he pleased to set.

"Now," he breathed to himself, "I can go my own way!"

The return voyage through space was uneventful. Several times, as the days wore on, the *Skylark* came within gravity-range of gigantic suns; but her pilots had learned the most important fundamental safeguard of interstellar navigation. Automatic indicating and recording goniometers were now on watch continuously, set to give alarm at a deviation of two seconds of arc; and their dead reckoning of acceleration and velocity was checked, twice each eight-hour shift, by triangulation and the application of Schuyler's Method.

When half the distance had been covered the bar was reversed, the travelers holding an impromptu ceremony as the *Skylark* spun through an angle of one hundred eighty degrees.

A few days later Seaton, who was on watch, thought he recognized Orion. It was by no means the constellation he had known, but it seemed to be shifting, ever so slowly, toward the old, familiar configuration. It *was* Orion!

"C'mere, everybody!" he shouted, and they came.

"That, my friends, is the most gladsome sight these feeble old eyes have rested on for many a long and weary moon. Wassail!"

They "wassailed" with glee, and from that moment on the pilot was never alone at his board. Everyone who could be there was there, looking over his shoulders to watch the firmament while it assumed a more and more familiar aspect.

They identified Sol; and, some time later, they could see Sol's planets.

Crane put on all the magnification he had, and the girls peered excitedly at the familiar outlines of continent and oceans upon the lighted half of the visible disk.

It was not long until these outlines were plainly visible to the unaided vision, the Earth appearing as a softly shining, greenish half-moon, with parts of its surface obscured by fleeecy wisps of cloud, with its ice-caps making of its poles two brilliant areas of white. The wanderers stared at their world with hearts in throats as Crane made certain that they would not be going too fast to land.

The girls went to prepare a meal and DuQuesne sat down beside Seaton.

"Have you gentlemen decided what you intend to do with me?"

"No. We haven't discussed it yet, and I can't make up my own mind—except that I'd like to have you in a square ring with four-ounce gloves. You've been of altogether too much real help on this trip for either of us to enjoy seeing you hanged. At the same time, you're altogether too much of a scoundrel for us to let you go free. . . . I, personally, don't like anything we can do, or not do, with you. That's the fix I'm in. What would you suggest?"

"Nothing," DuQuesne replied, calmly. "Since I am in no danger whatever of either hanging or prison, nothing you can say or do along those lines bothers me at all. Hold me or free me, as you please. I will add that, while I have made a fortune on this trip and do not have to associate any longer with Steel unless it is to my interest to do so, I may find it desirable at some future time to obtain a monopoly of X. If so, you and Crane, and possibly a few others, would die. No matter what happens or does not happen, however, this whole thing is over, as far as I'm concerned. Done with. *Fini.*"

"You kill us? You talk like a man with a paper nose. Peel off, buster, any time you like. We can outrun you, outjump you, throw you down, or lick you—hit harder, run faster, dive deeper and come up dryer—for fun, money, chalk, or marbles. . . ."

A thought struck him and every trace of levity disappeared. Face hard and eyes cold, he stared at DuQuesne, who stared unmovedly back at him.

"But listen, DuQuesne," Seaton said slowly, every word sharp, clear, and glacially cold. "That goes for Crane and me, personally. Nobody else. I could be arrested for what

I think of you as a man; and if anything you ever do touches either Dorothy or Margaret in any way I'll kill you like I would a snake—or rather, I'll take you apart like I would any other piece of scientific apparatus. And don't think this is a threat. It's a promise. Is that clear?"

"Perfectly. Good night."

For many hours Earth had been obscured by clouds, so that the pilot had no idea of what part of it was beneath them. To orient himself, Seaton dropped downward into the twilight zone until he could see the surface, finding that they were almost directly over the western end of the Panama Canal. Dropping still lower, to about ten thousand feet, he stopped and waited while Crane took bearings and calculated the course to Washington.

DuQuesne had retired, cold and reticent as usual. After making sure that he had overlooked nothing, he put on the leather suit he had worn when he left Earth. He unlocked a cubby, taking therefrom a Kondalian parachute. Then, making sure every foot of the way that he was not observed, he made his way to the airlock and entered it.

Thus, when the *Skylark* paused over the Isthmus, he was ready. Smiling sardonically, he opened the outer valve and stepped out into ten thousand feet of air. The neutral color of his parachute was lost in the twilight a few seconds after he left the vessel.

The course computed, Seaton set the bar and the *Skylark* tore through the air. When about half the ground had been covered Seaton spoke suddenly.

"Forgot about DuQuesne, Mart. We'd better lock him in, don't you think? Then we'll have to decide whether we want to put him in the jail-house or turn him loose."

"I'll see to it," Crane said.

He returned immediately with the news.

"Hmmm. He must have picked up a Kondalian parachute. You can't quite put one in your pocket, but pretty near. But I can't say I'm sorry he got away. . . . Anyway, we can get him any time we want him, because that compass is still looking right at him."

"I think he earned his liberty," Dorothy declared.

"He deserves to be shot," Margaret said, "but I'm glad he's gone. He gives me the cold, creeping shivers."

At the end of the calculated time they saw the lights of a large city beneath them; and Crane's fingers tightened upon Seaton's arm as he pointed downward. There were the landing-lights of Crane Field—seven searchlights throwing their mighty beams upward into the night.

"Nine weeks, Dick," he said unsteadily, "and Shiro would have kept them burning for nine years if necessary."

The Skylark dropped easily to the ground and the wanderers leaped out, to be greeted by the half-hysterical Japanese. Shiro's ready vocabulary of peculiar but sonorous words failed him completely and he bent himself double in a bow, his face one beaming smile. Crane, with one arm around his wife, seized Shiro's hand and wrung it in silence.

Seaton swept Dorothy off her feet and their arms tightened around each other.

THE END